THE BRIDE FROM ODESSA

EDGARDO COZARINSKY was born in Buenos Aires in 1939 and has lived in Paris since 1974. Best known for his subtle, semi-documentary films, he has also written a previous collection of short stories, *Urban Voodoo*, and prize-winning essays.

NICK CAISTOR's translations from the Spanish and Portuguese include the work of Juan Marsé, Eduardo Mendoza, Juan Carlos Onetti, Sergio Ramirez, José Saramago and Osvaldo Soriano.

Edgardo Cozarinsky

THE BRIDE FROM ODESSA

Translated from the Spanish by
Nick Caistor

THE HARVILL PRESS
LONDON

First published as *La novia de Odessa* by Emecé Editores S.A., Buenos Aires, 2001

2 4 6 8 10 9 7 5 3 1

Copyright © Edgardo Cozarinsky, 2001 © Emecé Editores S.A., Buenos Aires, 2001
English translation copyright © Nick Caistor, 2004

First published in Great Britain in 2004 by
The Harvill Press
Random House, 20 Vauxhall Bridge Road,
London SW1V 2SA

Random House Australia (Pty) Limited
20 Alfred Street, Milsons Point, Sydney,
New South Wales 2061, Australia

Random House New Zealand Limited
18 Poland Road, Glenfield,
Auckland 10, New Zealand

Random House (Pty) Limited
Endulini, 5A Jubilee Road, Parktown 2193, South Africa

The Random House Group Limited Reg. No. 954009
www.randomhouse.co.uk

A CIP catalogue record for this book
is available from the British Library

ISBN 1 84343051 7

Papers used by Random House are natural,
recyclable products made from wood grown in sustainable forests;
the manufacturing processes conform to the environmental
regulations of the country of origin

Designed and typeset in Spectrum by Palimpsest Book Production Limited,
Polmont, Stirlingshire
Printed and bound in Great Britain by Mackays of Chatham plc,
Chatham, Kent

For Alberto Tabbia

CONTENTS

THE BRIDE FROM ODESSA

ONE SPRING EVENING IN 1890, FROM HIS VANTAGE POINT UP
on the Primorksy Boulevard, a young man was watching the
movement of ships in the port of Odessa.

Decked out in his Sunday finest, he contrasted as much
with the everyday casualness of most of the passers-by as
with the exoticism of others. The fact is, the young man
was dressed to set out on a great adventure: his mother had
given him his varnished leather shoes; his uncle, a tailor by
trade, had completed his made-to-measure suit the day
before his departure; and finally, the hat he was wearing had
first been donned by his father on his wedding day twenty-
two years earlier, since when he had only had occasion to
wear it another five or six times.

At that moment the young man still had three days before
his big adventure really got underway, but to him the four
hundred versts from Kiev to Odessa, and this first sight of a
port and of the Black Sea (which would flow into the
Mediterranean, which in turn flowed into the Atlantic
Ocean) were part and parcel of the crossing that would make
a new man of him.

Yet a veil of sadness clouded the enthusiasm with which

he devoured all the sights of the big city and its port. Completely lacking any sentimental education, his one experience of love had troubled him so much it prevented him from enjoying the imminent realisation of his most daring project. In order to ward off this nagging feeling of loss, he stared intently at everybody who went by. There was something about each and every one of them that caught his attention: a nanny in starched uniform reluctantly pushing a perambulator, out of whose lacy frills poked a baby's ill-tempered head; two men whose bulging stomachs were signed with the flourish of the gold chains of invisible watches, as they strolled along discussing the prices of wheat and sunflowers on European markets; a black sailor, the first person he had seen of that colour, observing everything around him as curiously as he did himself; another sailor, who looked more like an actor dressed up to play the part, with a gold ear-ring and a parrot on his shoulder that he was trying unsuccessfully to sell.

A few yards beneath him on the pink granite Potemkin Steps, he spied a young girl staring at the landscape with a gaze every bit as melancholy as his own. She was sitting on one of the steps and had set down beside her two large round boxes, one on top of the other. Each one of them was done up with a blue satin ribbon, and they were held together with a simple piece of string. Written in Latin characters on the boxes were the words: "Madame Yvonne. Paris-Vienna-Odessa."

A pleasant breeze cooled the air, and far out to sea the fleeting forms of clouds shaped like dragons and archangels drifting from east to west seemed somehow to presage a happy encounter. The young man, whom we shall call Daniel Aisenson, did not know what words or gestures might allow him to introduce himself to an unknown woman. When she grew tired of pretending she had not noticed his presence, she cast him a stern glance, almost at once softened to a smile: something about him spoke of his innocence, a quality she had never encountered in any of the uncouth, or more refined seducers she had learnt to recognise in the big city.

We will never know what the first words they exchanged were, nor who uttered them, but it could well be she was the one who overcame the young man's shyness. Daniel was born in a *stetl*; when he was five, his parents had moved to a suburb in the holiest of all cities, Kiev, of which he knew little more than what was known as the Bessarabian market, and inside that, the family passementerie shop. As an adolescent, he had often paused to admire St Sophia cathedral's gold, spiralling columns, the five gleaming domes of the collegiate church of St Andrew, and taller still, the bell-tower of Petchersk monastery.

He could not help comparing the splendour of these monuments to the modest synagogue his parents attended without great conviction, and where he was obliged to accompany them. The comparison made him feel guilty. A divine injustice — he felt — had robbed him of an opulent, sheltering religion, and condemned him to an austere and cruel one, the natural corollary of which appeared to be the constant threat of pogrom: Cossacks had sliced his grandfather's legs off with a sabre slash when he had come forward to beg for mercy from the *hetman*; almost all his uncles had seen their houses burn, singled out by the six-pointed star which, despite being a sacred symbol, had marked them out for massacre rather than offering protection.

The young woman, whose name we shall never know, was by contrast a daughter of Odessa, where Greeks, Armenians, Turks and Jews were as common as Russians. She did not speak Ukrainian, but a rudimentary Russian, laced with a few words of Yiddish: despite not being Jewish herself, she lived and worked among Jews. Or rather, among Jewish women: the fearsome Madame Yvonne, whose real name was Rubi Guinzburg, and the three assistants who worked under her to create hats in a workshop on Deribassovska Street. They all came from the Moldavanka, but after years of strenuous effort, they had succeeded in distancing themselves in their imagination from this neighbourhood, although it was situated a mere ten streets from their workshop. Whenever there were no clients or suppliers in the shop, Yiddish rang out, used by Madame Yvonne to reproach or insult her girls, or by the latter to berate those ladies who tried on a dozen hats and left without buying a single one.

In this workshop, the young woman on the steps was the *shikse*, a ghastly word signifying both the servant and the non-Jew, the *goy*. The *shikse* had to clean the shop, prepare tea, take the hats to purchasers' houses, and carry out other errands and menial jobs. Her reward was a bed in the kitchen, a frugal meal, and the occasional tip at the tradesmen's entrance of a client.

* * *

The next evening saw the two of them sitting together on a bench under the acacias in Tchevchenko Park. The noise of the city was reduced to a murmur, and in the distance they could glimpse the sea and ships, a nebulous promise each of them interpreted as they saw fit.

She told him she was an orphan, and that thanks to studying the magazines from which Madame Yvonne copied her creations, she had learnt that life is the same in Paris, Vienna or Odessa, that without money all one can aspire to is a servant's life, and that the world is divided into haves and have-nots. He explained to her that this was true in Europe but that on the other side of the ocean there was a land of infinite possibilities, a young country where a Jew like him could hope to own a piece of land. Stumbling over his words, he told her about Baron Hirsch, about colonisation, Santa Fe, Entre Ríos. For the first time ever, she heard things she had never dreamt could exist: that a Jew could want to farm the soil, that he could fear Christians in the same way she feared the Jewish girls at the workshop, that he could talk to her about something other than the present he would give her if she agreed to spend the night with him in a cheap hotel on Privakzalnaia Square.

Can it have been during this second meeting that he revealed the apparently inexplicable reason for feeling such overwhelming sadness on the eve of his departure across the Atlantic in search of a new life? That reason had a name: Rifka Bronfman.

Their families had introduced them at the age of four-teen, having already betrothed them long before they met, and had married them five days before he left Kiev. Prior to their wedding, they had been alone together no more than ten times, always with parents or brothers and sisters in the adjoining room or spying at the window that looked out on the meagre garden that separated house from street.

Daniel had begun toying with the idea of emigrating a year earlier. On a visit to Kiev, the delegation of Jewish Colonisation for Argentina had organised evening meetings in the Israeli Mutual Association. With the help of a magic lantern and a dozen glass plates, an eloquent speaker had shown them the endless fertile plains of Argentina that awaited them. He had indicated where these lands were, and their distance from the main cities: Buenos Aires and Rosario, which they had seen in other plates. He had also waved a slender publication bound in sky-blue and white in which — he explained — were printed the words (in Spanish, and therefore in Latin characters) "Constitution of the Argentine Republic". From this tome he had read, translating himself instantaneously into Yiddish, those articles which promised equality before the law and freedom of worship for all those willing to work in this "land of peace".

Daniel had repeated these words to Rifka; he described the images in great detail. His fiancée did not share his enthusiasm. In accordance with the precept that a woman's place is by her husband's side, she agreed to follow him, but this new world did not haunt her dreams. When he filled out the necessary papers, she made no specific objection, but when they came back duly approved and stamped by the Argentine consulate, and she read there her name, date of birth, the colour of her hair and eyes, she burst into violent sobs which, just as it seemed they must give way to exhaustion, broke out afresh . The two families decided it must be a nervous condition brought on by the proximity of her wedding; a cousin who had vaguely studied medicine informed them it was a very fashionable complaint known as neurasthenia. Pleased with this diagnosis, Rifka endured the service in the synagogue with great dignity, beneath the ritual wig that covered her freshly shaven head.

That night, Daniel had to overcome his inexperience, and Rifka her fear. Amid the bleeding, he found pleasure; she discovered pain. The next morning he woke up alone in bloody sheets; in the distance he could hear shouts, tears, reproaches, complaints. He saw Rifka in the arms of his mother-in-law, refusing to be comforted. While the older woman tried to drown out the young bride's protests by repeating over and over "She'll get over it, she'll get over it", Rifka succeeded in making heard what she was shouting with ever greater insistence: "I'm not going, I'm not going, I'm not going". When she had calmed down a little, she was able to string a few words together and explain:

"I'm afraid, very afraid. I know everyone here, this is where my family is from, and your family, and my girlfriends; this is where the synagogue is, the market, everything I know. What are we going to find over there? Snakes? Indians? Carnivorous plants?"

Daniel tried to tell her that she now had a husband who could protect her, but Rifka seemed deaf to all argument. When she finally managed to dry her tears, she accepted, together with a glass of tea and more sugar than lemon, the barely optimistic, almost despairing suggestion her mother made: that she should travel a year, or perhaps only six months after her husband, once he had written to confirm she would be safe from all the perils the novels of Emilio Salgari had conjured up for her.

During the remaining nights before he set out, Daniel refrained from touching her. Perhaps secretly relieved, Rifka did not hold it against him.

* * *

The young woman has been listening to him in silence. They have walked from the park to the scene of their first encounter. The pink evening sky has gradually given way to an increasingly deep blue. Night has fallen by the time he finishes his rushed, jumbled story, which the preceding paragraphs have attempted to summarise.

They walk past cafés and patisseries with French and Italian names they cannot permit themselves to enter. Behind the lace curtain of one of the windows, she recognises the linen flowers, the embalmed and stitched bird, and the silk ribbons of a hat she saw being created piece by piece, and which now crowns an invisible head. They reach the statue of a French duke whose name means nothing to them; it is lit by the feeble, fitful glow from the windows of the London Hotel. In the distance, the ships anchored in the harbour also cast random reflections across the black, whispering waters.

When she speaks at last, it is not to comment on the tale she has listened to so attentively.

"When do you embark?"

"Tomorrow. The ship leaves at six in the evening, but the third-class passengers have to be on board by noon."

She stares at him, expecting words that do not come. After a moment's pause, she insists.

"Are you intending to travel alone?"

He stares back at her, catching her meaning but scarcely daring to believe he has properly understood.

"Alone . . . Why, what other choice do I have . . . ?"

She seizes him by the arms, blocking his path. Daniel can sense that these small hands can grip and perhaps even hit out, that they are not made simply to wield a needle.

"Take me with you! I could pass for blonde, I have light eyes even if they are not blue, I am only just under a metre sixty-five, and I am eighteen! Is there a photograph in that safe-conduct of yours?"

"But . . ." he manages to stammer out, "we're not married . . ."

Her peal of laughter rings out across the deserted square, seems to roll down the steps and echo out over the harbour.

"How could we be married if I'm an Orthodox Russian and you're a Jew! It would take months before a rabbi accepted my conversion . . . and anyway, didn't you say that in this new country of yours, nothing of what keeps us slaves here has any importance? Let's go together!"

As Daniel looks on dumbfounded, she starts spinning round, arms outstretched, like an Anatolian dervish. Laughing all the while, she repeats like an incantation the names she has heard mentioned only a few moments before.

"Buenos Aires! Rosario! Entre Ríos! Santa Fe! Argentina!"
She laughs louder and louder, and spins on and on.
"I am Rifka Bronfman!"

* * *

One hundred and ten years after this scene, while he is convalescing in a Paris hospital, this couple's great-grandson receives a letter from his Aunt Draifa in Buenos Aires. In it, "feeling the moment of departure drawing closer every day", the old lady tells him this story, a secret passed down by the women of the family, the eldest in each generation revealing it only to the eldest of the next. The aunt has chosen him because geographical distance seems to guarantee the secret will be kept, while allowing her to keep the promise of passing it on.

While he waits for the results of a second biopsy on his spine, he lets his memory drift back to the snippets he had heard as a boy about the great-grandfather he had never known, and of the mother of ten children born in Argentina who was that young woman, who one spring evening in 1890 sat staring sadly at the ships leaving the port of Odessa.

He had inherited a picturesque image of his great-grandfather as a womaniser, a bit of a wastrel: an image derived, he now understands, from the episode his Aunt Draifa has revealed to him in her letter. But on the other hand, could it not be said to have been simply commonsense to forget a woman who was too frightened to cross the Atlantic, and replace her with someone else whose courage and daring he was sure to have need of?

He knew that this great-grandmother Rifka, whose real

name no-one ever knew, was both courageous and daring. In 1902, on the farm, two well-aimed bullets from her pistol had accounted for a pair of gypsy prowlers, known as child snatchers throughout the region of Gualeguay. In 1904, after having borne a child every year, she accepted a tenth pregnancy against the advice of Doctor Averbuch, who had attended all her births. She gave birth to a girl as blonde as she was, with the same light-coloured eyes, only to die a few hours later of puerperal fever.

All at once her great-grandson understands why instead of feeling proud of this ancestor of theirs, the women of the family, or at least those charged with transmitting the secret, had passed down the information as if it were a piece of dangerous, perhaps forbidden, knowledge. It was not that they were worried by any absurd ideas of illegitimacy or fraud; but, according to the Talmudic law, to be a Jew passes down through the mother's line, and therefore the ten children of that marriage were not Jewish . . .

The hospital patient, who forty-eight hours later is to learn how long he has left to live, thinks about his father and mother. Just where had their belonging to the "chosen" race ended and begun again? (That word "chosen" seems more than ever to him to be surrounded by a dark, sinister halo.) Brought up without religion, for him that continuity had not been expressed by any mystical tie or consoling tradition, but only through occasional gastronomic outings. And of course, by the "shitty Russian" heard at primary school, as well as by the frequency of guard and latrine duties he had endured during his military service.

But he is too weary to feel sorry for himself. His thoughts turn instead to a faceless person, to the real Rifka Bronfman, the one who preferred the illusion of safety with family and friends. If she was twenty in 1890, she must have been around sixty in 1941 . . . Did she die at Babi Yar? If she was still alive at the time of the German invasion, which most Ukrainians welcomed as liberation from the Soviet yoke, she might have been dispatched by a Wehrmacht *Einsatzgruppe*, or by the SS, or by a gang of nationalists, possibly even her neighbours; people who had always been so smiling and friendly, but who suddenly now were enemies, zealous seekers of justice intent on uprooting the Semitic weed from the garden of the fatherland.

He also reflects that he has no children, does not even know the distant offspring of so many cousins scattered throughout the world by fresh winds of want and fear. He realises no-one is going to call him to account for not passing on this piece of family history. But two days later, on an impulse he would be hard put to explain, he starts to write it as a story.

LITERATURE

THE FIRST THING MY AUNT IGNACIA ALWAYS TURNED TO IN the newspapers was the obituaries. During my know-all adolescent years, I sneered at this habit of hers. Her life seemed to me so entirely lacking in incident that it could offer no possibility of having made the kind of enemies whose death, one supposes, is the always deferred, nearly always frustrated, satisfaction of this daily ritual.

Then, one morning many years later, I found myself searching among the death notices for the rebuttal of a dream: during the night I had twice discovered my own name in this section as someone who had died, and in the same item, as the only relative of the deceased. I did not find my own name, but my relief was short-lived when instead I came across that of Natalia Safna Dolgoruki.

This combination of in themselves unremarkable syllables produced in me the effect of a musical chord resonating to infinity. Above and beyond her features, which I could no longer clearly distinguish, I was overcome by a jumbled mass of images: of myself, still young, of friends and places in a Buenos Aires that was dead and gone, which I believed buried out of reach of memory, a scar barely visible among all the banal wrinkles etched by time.

The notice said that a memorial service to commemorate the tenth anniversary of her death was to be held that afternoon. It was to take place at the Russian Orthodox church in the Calle Brasil, the same one whose domes, so exotic in Buenos Aires, I had glimpsed like huge golden onions between the foliage whenever my mother took me for walks in Lezama Park in my early years.

So, half a century later, I was about to penetrate for the first time into this darkness perfumed by distant incense, I was going to glimpse the absent gazes of unknown saints by the reddish light of the hanging lamps, amidst all the gold of the iconostasis . . .

As I came up from the Paseo Colón, I already noticed one incongruity: the five domes crowned with crosses — a large one in the middle, and four at the corners — were painted a sky-blue colour. Had they always been that way, while I had superimposed on them the image of more opulent churches I had seen later on in life? Or was it a recent cheap remedy, aimed at disguising the damage suffered by the original gilt? On the left-hand portico wall, a mural in polychrome tiles celebrated the millennium of the "baptism of Russia (988-1988)"; the fact that it had been put up so recently would perhaps explain why, despite its lack of any Renaissance perspective, it reminded me of the art on biscuit-tin lids.

Stepping inside the church, I decided to keep what I thought to be a respectful distance from the only three people in the first row of pews: to the left, a married couple of uncertain years, dressed with studied care; on the right, a gentleman of incalculable age, less scrupulously dressed, but with one splendidly anachronistic detail that made me instantly think of him as a character: a pince-nez balanced in the regulation way on his bony nose, with a thin black velvet ribbon hanging to the side. On a second inspection, the female of the couple I had perhaps somewhat hastily considered to be man and wife was also wearing something remarkable: a small purple "pillbox" hat, complete with a short veil of the same colour.

It was enough for the invisible Russian Orthodox priest to launch into his resonant prayers for Natalia Safna for me to become immersed in the only life my memory could offer her. "The Russky woman", as we Argentine friends used to call her, with as much respect as familiarity, had for years been an infallible reference point for a literature I was fascinated by, but was unable to read in the original. (Fascinated perhaps because I could not read it in the original?) Three afternoons a week, in her tiny one-bedroom apartment at the corner of Caseros and Piedras, I read out aloud translations of Russian novels in Spanish, French and English, while she read them silently in their original language. From time to time she would burst out laughing; though invariably she was lenient towards the translator's mistakes, or easy approximations, her only comment being a sympathetic and sonorous "poorr thing!", rolling the "r" deep in her throat with great pleasure. Without making any great show of knowledge, she would then proceed to correct the translation: she recognised the difficulties and forgave the transgressors with a simple "they trried but got it wrrong". Following which, more often than not, she would embark on an explanation of the context of the work, throwing open unsuspected windows on the life of the imaginary continent which Russia was for me.

It might be the exact colour of the stocking that Prince Hippolitus wears in the third chapter of the first book of *War and Peace*, which Tolstoy defines in French as *"cuisse de nymphe effrayée"*, and which may be an ineffable shade of pink and apricot. It might be a short aside to inform me that Chekhov's two dogs in his Melikhovo residence were called Bromide and Quinine. It could also be a short geography lesson to explain where remote regions of the Caucasus like Ossetia, Daghestan and Chechenia were. At the time for me they were no more than the backdrop for Pushkin's exile or for Lermontov's "hero of our time"; back then I had no notion that at the end of the twentieth century they would become notorious for their civil wars, rival mafias and illegal emigration.

I would guess that the modest sum I used to leave at the first of our monthly meetings — in an envelope under the tea tray that never interrupted the conversation — was enough only to help ease the difficulties of each month's end for this solitary woman whose only relatives appeared to be Turgenev, Chekhov, Tolstoy, Dostoevksy or, their incomparable forebear, Pushkin. ("Don't even bother trying to read him in translation, he can only be appreciated in Russian.") Natasha Safna was not unaware of more recent authors: one day she mentioned Biely, another time she spoke of Nabokov, calling him Sirin, the pseudonym he published under in Berlin and Paris, and whom, I understood, she had met through her Jewish friend Vera Slonim.

Even though she never talked about it, the "Russky's" past was not impenetrable. It was enough not to ask about it for her to allow a few glimmers to shine through the dark curtain of literature. A photograph I paused to examine on a bookshelf drew the brief comment: "it's no-one, only a cousin". And then, in a whisper: "*Il faisait le danseur au Touquet, en* 1932 . . ." On another occasion, she corrected my impression of Istanbul being a hot city: "It snows a lot in winter on the Bosphorus . . .", adding by way of justification: "We lived there between 1920 and 1926."

I was particularly struck by the animosity she felt towards England. This anger did not of course prevent her from admiring the poetry of Donne and Keats, which she often quoted in the original with perfect pronunciation, or Hawksmoor churches and the paintings of Gainsborough; but she spoke equally often of "perfidious Albion" with a firmness that did not change if she said it in French or Spanish as well. One day she reproached me with a smile: "anglophile, like so many Argentines . . ." I was never able to explain to her, in my jejeune way, that for me anglophobia was synonymous with an Argentina of pericón dances, offal, and scarlet emblems that threatened me with phrases like "rope sandals yes, books no" heard in childhood: an inhospitable land where the local neighbourhood overseer could betray you, a land far, far distant from the prose of a Julio Irazusta.

Beyond the Russia written about and read, even in unfaithful translations, that formed the basis of our relationship, there sprawled an Argentina that seemed to me both monotonous and colourless. Terrible years were brewing there, but at that time, its reality seemed to me immeasurably inferior to the fiction in which I was immersed. Its daily newspapers were filled with the clamour of vile military men, crapulous trade unionists, demented guerillas, but none of these left the slightest trace in my imagination.

Bit by bit I stopped seeing the "Russky", for paltry reasons I am now ashamed of. Her deafness, for example. Since she could not disguise it, she thought she could remedy it by using an archaic hearing-aid powered by batteries contained in a silver metal case clipped like a brooch onto her blouse. And looking back, I can see that I was guilty of being caught up in a present whose protagonists and events now seem to me desolately trivial. I learnt of her death when I returned to Buenos Aires after a trip abroad; I never knew where she was buried, or what had happened to her Russian books and poor flaking icons.

* * *

At the end of the service, during which I was the only one not to take communion, when we had gone out into the street, I was the object of stern, perhaps disapproving, glances from the other three. It was plain that more than simply being unknown, I was an intruder. The elderly couple made short work of their farewells, and headed off towards the Calle Defensa, walking laboriously but steadily up the slope;

18

for his part, the old gentleman displayed unexpected vigour in hailing a taxi, which he then got into with some difficulty. Two minutes later and they had all disappeared from my sight, no doubt to return to that ghostly existence of emigrés "whose only hope and only profession is their past" (Nabokov).

Opposite me, the Lezama Park seemed less green, far dustier than I remembered it. On its now garishly painted stone steps, a dark-skinned destitute family was sharing out hunks of bread and cold sausage, using the wrapping paper as tablecloth. Further off, under the trees, I caught the sickly smell of rotting vegetation. It was only when I saw a group of no longer young men and women decked out in faded clothes all the colours of the rainbow, that I recognised the smell as the mixture of pachuli and cannabis that had been so popular in the days of hippies. These pathetic survivors of that time were displaying bead necklaces of wire, glass and tin, presumably to fulfil the regulations some municipal authority had established for so-called craft fairs. The only thing missing was the necessary counterpart: someone willing to purchase these unappealing trinkets.

I reflected that I might just have spent an hour in the company of people from another time and place, but that they at least had given me the glimpse of some germ of fiction. They aroused curiosity, not compassion.

Two days later, the phantoms came knocking at my door again: in the post I received a small package containing a letter and a book. The former, signed with an illegible scrawl, was written in a highly formal French. Its author explained to me that shortly before her death "our friend Natasha Safna" had asked that, if I should ever materialise one day, I was to be given the book. Ten years had gone by, and my absence and silence had been complete, until two days previously . . .

Who was this man who not only knew my name and address, but was sufficiently aware of my appearance to be able to identify me in the Calle Brasil church? Which of the people I had glimpsed that afternoon was the first person masculine singular who had written these lines?

The book was an Everyman Library edition of John Keats' poetry. It took me back to a time which, being that of my youth, I was determined not to consider far-off, a time when a popular English edition of a book could have a hard binding and a decent cover. The book opened by itself at the page of *Ode on a Grecian Urn*, thanks to the pressure of several folded sheets of that thin paper used in former days for airmail letters. These sheets were covered with tiny writing in Russian, and dated from the year 1946. My modest knowledge of the Cyrillic script did not allow me to go much further than the initial "Daragoia Natasha Safna". The writing paper was as translucent and fragile as a butterfly's wings, and seemed about to disintegrate between my fingers. I decided to protect the sheets in transparent plastic folders and to photocopy them. Who could help me? I made so bold as to turn to Alejo Flor´n-Christensen.

A few days later, I received the photocopy I had sent him together with the following translation. They were accompanied by a letter in which my friend spoke of his fear of being unable to capture in Spanish "the profoundly moving tone" of the Russian text.

Plättling, in Bavaria
February 1946

Dear Natasha Safna,

This may well be the last letter I write, and I take no pleasure from it. I am writing at the request of my best friend: your brother Piotr Aleksandrovich. They took him away yesterday, and I do not expect to see him again. Since Germany's surrender, we have been through several prison camps without anyone ever explaining our situation. We know exactly what it is, however. In February last year, at the Yalta Conference, Churchill and Roosevelt gave in to Stalin and not only handed him the eastern half of Europe, but also promised him our lives . . . of course, nothing as dramatic as this has ever been admitted. The operation is called "Repatriation", even though I need not remind you that none of us has ever been a citizen of the Soviet Union. Some of the older men among us fought under Krasnov when England and France entered Russia by the port of Murmansk in 1919. (Murmansk! Five months of night and temperatures of minus 50 degrees . . .) We should have learnt something from that first defeat. But we didn't. How many of us were there: a hundred, a hundred and fifty thousand, who followed the Wehrmacht in 1941 in the belief we were going to liberate our country from the Bolsheviks? It seems that at Yalta Stalin was particularly keen to get us back . . .

You cannot imagine, Natasha Safna, the exodus of Russians and Ukrainians that followed the German army's retreat: whole families trudging on foot along the snowy roads, sometimes with an old grandmother on a cart, people who had never used a weapon, as we had, people who never "collaborated with the invader" as the Americans say . . . (The Americans! A nation which has never been invaded or occupied, which has always fought its wars on foreign soil . . .) People desperate to seize this one last chance they were being offered to escape from the Soviet Union. I have no illusions about what awaits us. At first we were kept nearby, in Dachau. When we were taken there we were surprised that although there were no trees in the camp, the ground was strewn with yellow leaves . . . I picked one up. It was a cloth star, and written on it in Gothic script was the word "Jew" . . . all the Jews held in the camp had been liberated a fortnight earlier. Now they have brought us to Plättling, and we have not been able to sleep for five days. Every morning before sunrise American soldiers come into our bunkhouses and beat on the metal legs of the beds with their baseball bats, shouting in poor German *"Mach schnell!"* until we are all lined up outside in the snow of the yard. Every day they pick out forty or fifty prisoners and put them on trucks to travel to the Czech border, where a Red Army division is waiting for them . . . In Dachau, eight of our officers committed suicide, and here Commander Samoilov opened a wound in his chest by rubbing against the barbed wire . . . the Americans' only reaction was to film him before they took him off to hospital . . . I'll be one of the last, because they need me as an interpreter . . . See where our childhood reading has got us . . . *Lyrisches Intermezzo, Tom Brown's Schooldays* . . . yesterday when he came back from the Czech frontier, an American NCO noticed our expressions and burst into tears. He was like a child. He kept on stammering about "trees covered with hanged men, right there in the wood . . ." General Krasnov, always a man of the old school, sent a message to Churchill reminding Sir Winston that in 1918 he had decorated him with the British Military Cross . . . can he really be expecting a reply? Can he think it's possible? From the English? The English, who early last year bombed Dresden when it was not a military target, destroying Germany's most beautiful city and killing hundreds of thousands of refugees from the East who had managed to get there . . . (and of the Americans it's said here that they have exploded a new weapon on a Japanese city, a bomb whose destructive power is beyond belief.) *Vous avez été épargnée,* you have been spared, dear Natasha Safna, and it is not my intention in writing these lines to darken what I imagine to be tranquil days in that

far-off corner of the earth. I wonder whether, as well
as informing you of our Piotr Aleksandrovich's fate, I
wanted to leave some trace, to throw a bottle into
the sea. (Will this letter ever reach you? I'll entrust it
to the American NCO; he's the only one who has
shown us any sympathy.) We are the great — the only
— losers. We're not important to anyone, nobody
needs us. The Germans are essential to Europe; the
United States and the Soviet Union will patch up
their wounds, re-educate them, and use them until
the day they again become the strongest, and shake
off all their pimping godfathers
. . . They say here that the American secret services,
who like businessmen know what's going to happen
tomorrow before the politicians in Washington get
wind of it, are already recruiting the heads of the
Nazi spy system to get hold of their files on Soviet
spy rings; they will keep them in Canada for a while
under false names, then greet them in their Eldorado
of hot dogs and Coca-Cola. (This is a dark, sticky
cordial we were given when we first got here, as if it
were from a delicatessen; it seems it's very popular
with young people on the other side of the ocean.)
As for the Jews, you know I never despised them like
so many of our people did, those who felt they
deserved the concentration camps for having made
the Russian Revolution . . . one of the few things I
have learnt from these terrible years is that there is no
such thing as collective guilt, there are only individual

crimes, which some of us allow ourselves, and others
forbid themselves, and which perhaps we only
commit for self-protection . . . the Jews, as I was
saying, the ones who have survived hell, are trying by
every possible means to get to their Promised Land.
At the moment it's occupied by the English, the
same people who in the words of that idiot Lord
Balfour promised them a "national homestead" in
Palestine, back in the tragic year of 1918 . . . His
Majesty's fleet is currently blockading the Palestine
ports to stop the Jews disembarking . . . but for how
long? The future belongs to the Americans and the
Soviets, the days of the British Empire are numbered
. . . Just like us . . . for many, many years I dreamt of
seeing Russia again, and in my dreams I was a little
boy once more, playing in the snow at Tsarskoie Sielo
. . . Sometimes I wonder if I ever was that boy, or if I
dreamt the whole thing, if it is only a "figment of my
imagination", literature that is bad because it is not
written or read, but searched for in real life . . . If I'm
not shot first, I will get to see my, our, promised
land, but only for a very short while . . . will you
forgive me, dear Natasha Safna, for having sent you
these rambling thoughts, this petty unburdening, for
spilling my bitterness and fear over you? May our
Lord bless you, may Saint Basil protect you until the
end of your days.

Yours ever,

ANDREI DIMITROVICH

Reading the letter, or rather its translation, left me unmoved, as if anaesthetized, for several minutes. I would have liked to have read more. I tried rereading the sheets of paper, but abandoned the attempt after the first few lines. Apathy, fatigue, fear? I put down the translation and the photocopies and went to look for the original, as if I needed to check that it had really existed. Under their plastic cover, the transparent sheets looked as if they were about to disappear altogether, as if any fresh contact with the air might be fatal. I tried to imagine the face of the man who had written the letter: a futile exercise which simply led me once more to the blurred memory I had of Natasha Safna's features.

I smiled an inappropriate smile: I could not help thinking that "our friend" – wherever she may be at this century's end – would have been pleased to witness the banal rather than sordid decadence of the country she had chosen to hate. Perhaps she would have averted her eyes, with a morally elegant gesture, to avoid seeing, in the midst of the financial splendour engineered by Baroness Thatcher, the worn-out remains of a royalty only capable of appealing to its people thanks to the accidental death of an adulterous, cocaine-sniffing princess and her incidental Egyptian beau.

The Everyman's Library volume was still in my hands, and was still open at the *Ode on a Grecian Urn*. Someone – the Russky? – had underlined in pencil its last two verses:

> *"Beauty is truth, truth beauty" – that is all*
> *Ye know on earth, and all ye need to know.*

Many years earlier, I had learnt those lines by heart, and

thought I knew what they meant. Now I re-read them as if for the first time. They seemed to me ironical, with an irony Keats never intended, but which History had stealthily deposited on them, like a thin film of ashes, aimed at me and me alone.

REAL ESTATE

MY BROTHER IS NOT LIKE ME. NOT AT ALL. I KNOW I SHOULD say my "half brother" but I find the term comical: it reminds me of the childhood magician who sawed in half a box in which a scantily clad girl with ample thighs and an inviting smile had stretched out without the slightest fear or hesitation. (And who had emerged a few minutes later following the strenuous efforts of her sweaty accomplice, sporting an even broader, more inviting smile, and bowed to the public's applause.) Neither I nor my brother, however much we are considered "halves" in legal phraseology, has ever in any imaginable past been a single, unique person; not even in the womb of the mother who conceived us, by different fathers, eight years apart. I call him brother out of politeness, even though I am not sure that it matters to him. Perhaps I do so as a vague gesture, whose meaning escapes me, towards that woman who was to vanish from his life just as a few years earlier she had disappeared from mine.

I watch him preparing the *mate* tea, tamping down the leaves, making sure the water does not go off the boil. He is sitting on a small bench in front of the brazier; he has motioned me towards a folding metal chair that looks unstable and which, as far as I can tell, does not get much use. In the shade of the eaves at the back of the house, the afternoon heat seems bearable, although the sun is still beating down on fields that are not so much unattended as left to invade what once must have been a vegetable garden. But for the moment my interest is focussed on him.

"You haven't changed your mind?"

He gives a low laugh, as if my question cannot have been serious, or as if it calls for a jocular response.

"Why do you ask when you know I haven't?"

It's true, I know he does not want to leave this dump which cannot mean anything to him, because it does not even mean much to me. My offer is a very reasonable one: to sell the land, however low prices are at the moment, with the house included — after all, it is a ruin that only he considers inhabitable. I would look after everything, not even charge my commission, then split the proceeds equally between us. I try to soften him by talking openly.

"There's something I don't understand. How much younger are you than me? Eight, ten years? You're still young. Fine: I can understand you don't want to be an engineer. But . . . burying yourself alive here . . . is there nothing in the world that interests you? I'm not talking about a job, I'm talking about choosing somewhere that's not so sad, so desolate . . ."

His smile broadens still further, although he has stopped laughing. He says nothing, and the smile freezes into a grimace.

"What can I say? . . . That's life."

* * *

When he had reached Gualeguay that morning, Ariel Verefkin had thought he might find a taxi to take him to the house: it was only twenty kilometres from town, and it looked like being a dry day.

(He remembered a frustrated journey his father had dragged him on as a boy, in the decrepit 1938 Chrysler he still refused to be parted with in the 1950s. "Look, a good old car is better than one of those tin cans they make in Argentina these days." His aim had been to show him the place where his grandparents had settled when they arrived from an unimaginable country called Bessarabia. Ariel, at that time an avid consumer of the Robin Hood collection of comics and of Fox Cinemascope films, could see nothing that might interest him in the trip. No sooner had they left Gualeguay than the rain turned the dirt road into a mudslide; the noble Chrysler got stuck and a garage truck had to use chains to tow them back to the paved road on the outskirts of town.)

But this morning the town was reeling from the noise of a national bikers' convention: about five hundred of them were parked outside the public lido, while he spent forty minutes in the Monte Carlo bar, where they promised to call him a taxi or to find someone to take him. But no rescuing car had materialised. His commercial instinct told him they were keeping him waiting so that he would consume more, but he soon had to accept the fact that they had simply forgotten him: the bar owner and the waiters had joined the few customers in the doorway to talk to all the strangers who were parking their bikes outside: roaring monsters that in a few minutes were strangely transformed into silent metal sculptures.

Gradually he felt himself being swept up in this general curiosity. He was surprised at his own lack of reticence: here he was, someone who did not usually let himself be distracted from his professional duties (and this was after all, he told himself, a professional visit), yet he began to find himself drawn into this spontaneous spectacle. Hollywood films had led him to associate this kind of get-together with the terror of apocalyptic gangs: fat, greasy Vietnam veterans covered in tattoos and somehow both bald and hairy; raunchy but submissive women clinging to their leather-lined backs; all of it under the sign of copious drugs and the occasional swastika. Here, however, he found himself faced with affable youngsters who had decorative beards and ears pierced with completely unthreatening rings; even the myth-ical beasts of their tattoos were more fantastic than terrifying. The atmosphere of their convention, Ariel thought, was not too dissimilar to that of those trips to Bariloche organised by schoolkids who have just done their final exams . . .

Somewhere in the smiling, talkative crowd milling around the bikers must be his taxi-driver or the car owner anxious to earn a few extra pesos, whose services he had been rather too quick to dismiss . . . while he was pondering this, a buzz of voices led everyone to peer towards one corner of the square. Several bikes set off and formed a guard of honour for a dust-covered Toyota making its triumphal entry. It was ridden by a tall, skinny figure, one arm raised in acknow-ledgement.

"It's Granny Toyota!" youthful voices exclaimed.

Greeted by this wave of affection, the bike was forced to a halt, to be immediately surrounded by lots of Nissans and Harley-Davidsons, Honda Rebels and Varaderos, even by more modest Gileras. The helmet was lifted off to reveal the wrinkled, sunburnt face and cropped white hair of a radiant old woman.

* * *

No, my brother is nothing like me. His name is Hugo Acuña, and I reckon he hasn't worked a day in his life, apart from dreaming up ways to allow him to live without working. This spoilt brat must have some money in the bank, otherwise he could not afford to buy the *mate* tea he drinks all day long, or feed the horse he goes out for a ride on every morning. What leads a thirty-five-year-old man, educated in Europe and with a university degree, to come and bury himself alive on this piece of land that my grandfather and his brothers could not wait to escape from?

But I am not here to analyse his behaviour. I am here to value the house and the land where once the family tried to grow sunflowers and later, when the fields would no longer produce them, rice. It seems that the annual appearance of locusts, which turned the sky black in only a few minutes, and took even less time to strip all the trees bare, plus the way my grandmother and her sisters beat on any metal container they had to hand, making an enormous din that should have scared off the locusts but rarely did, were enough for a whole generation to choose city life instead. In fact, the city is the only thing that links me to all those doctors, accountants and dentists who offered so many diplomas to the satisfaction of their parents. I buy and sell properties, and although at the real estate agency the secretary calls me "doctor", I do not have any university degree.

I look at the house: the main block built from adobe, which they tried to smarten up with a stucco covering that has mostly peeled off, and another block built of brick which was added on some years later when the fourth child appeared. In both parts, the floor was, is, of beaten earth. The kitchen is at the back, and opens onto the fields. A hundred yards further off, a little shed contains the toilet. The land registry mentions a hectare of land, but even if the fields, which have not been planted in many years, could be cultivated again, even if the ruined old shack of a home could be demolished to make way for a proper house, even if the road out here, which is no longer a dirt road but is made-up, could be asphalted, the *coup de grâce* as far as its real estate value goes comes from the fact that to one side of the house, 150 yards away but adjoining the property, stands what once used to be Baron Hirsch's school. There have been no pupils here for years: the provincial health authority took over the two buildings to install Doctor Marcos Trachtenberg's lunatic asylum. They say that at nightfall, when they let the inmates out into the yard to stretch their legs, their voices, curses and obscene laughter carry over the high wall separating the two properties. This is the unsaleable real estate that thanks to our inheritance laws I share with Hugo Acuña, whom I am kind enough to call brother.

★ ★ ★

Ariel Verefkin will not give up. Sitting with a beer in the relative cool of the Monte Carlo, he surveys the motorbikes covering the field known as the Planta de Campamento: they look like huge immobile cockroaches, which their masters and slaves have washed before they take part in the parade in the Gualeguay Corsódromo; without the dust of the road on them, they gleam in the afternoon sun. At a neighbouring table, "Granny Toyota" is explaining to two bearded young men wearing identical rings on the fingers of their right hands the need to take a mobile phone with them, especially if they are travelling on such dangerous roads as those in Chubut and La Pampa.

But these characters and their conversation do not distract Ariel. More than once he has thought he should forget the property: even if a buyer did appear, the price he could get for it would be ridiculous, and as his father used to say, "fifty per cent of ridiculous is pathetic". But he also thinks that this is the one way finally to get Hugo Acuña out of his life. Simply by existing, Hugo reminds him that his mother left him and his father to run off with a man called Acuña, well known in the casino at the Rio Hondo spa; that a short while afterwards she had followed Acuña to Spain when his business interests led him to Barcelona; that she had given birth to this same Hugo there, who years later, after his mother had mysteriously disappeared, had chosen not merely to come back to Argentina, but to live in this corner of Entre Ríos that had nothing to do with him or his history, this Hugo Acuña who now wore rope sandals and drank *mate*, and looked as ridiculous as those middle-class kids who a few decades earlier had shaved their heads, wrapped themselves in saffron-coloured robes, and paraded the streets chanting "Hare Krishna" . . .

One summer night, when Ariel was still very small, his father had cleared the table after dinner and called his son to witness a private ceremony. For half an hour, perhaps more, he had proceeded to obliterate every image he could find of his wife in the apartment. Painstakingly, the scissors separated her image from that of anyone else she shared a photograph with; when the image was on its own, he cut it up in every direction: vertically, horizontally. Ariel could see bits that survived: here a smile, there a gaze, elsewhere, a wave of the hand. Stripped of their context, these fragments were open to endless interpretation, and acquired fresh meanings. Rather than a long-since faded presence, warmth, voice, it is these fragments of a body, their varied and multiple mutilation, that Ariel remembers of his mother: without nostalgia, almost without rancour. If the house and land were sold, he wants to believe, nothing would be left to remind me of her, not even the demands for local property taxes that arrive at my office every twelve months like an unwelcome birthday present.

He decides to give it one last try. Among the most enthusiastic people welcoming the bikers, he recognises the owner of the Renault who a few hours earlier had been his driver. It is not difficult to convince him, for the same price, to repeat his journey, wait for him ("it'll be no more than half an hour, I promise you") then bring him back to Gualeguay before nightfall.

36

By the time the car pulls up at the roadside a few yards from the house, the pink clouds are turning a deeper red and unravelling in an increasingly intense blue sky. A weary dog comes out to greet him, sniffing at his muddy shoes. It has cataracts in its left eye, and stays beside him as he walks into the empty house and gazes round it without calling to Hugo. They finally emerge from the cool of the house into the open kitchen, whose tin roof no longer offers any protection from the accumulated heat of the long day. The metal chair and bench are where they were three hours earlier, as are the kettle and the *mate* gourd. The dog watches Ariel come and go with quiet resignation. In the distance, the open privy door signals there is no-one in there either. The horse, loosely tethered to a weeping willow, appears unaware of any visitor.

As if for the first time, Ariel listens to the breeze rustling the grass in the fields, a breeze that carries with it the discordant sounds of invisible birds, and promises to bring some evening coolness. At this hour, when the day is slipping rapidly away, and the light bestows unfamiliar colours on this well-known landscape, Ariel feels that time is standing still. This ruined house and sterile plot of land no longer threaten him as tokens of a past he has tried to eradicate; on the contrary, he suddenly understands they could have their enchantment, even if he cannot see it and is only just beginning to accept that it exists.

Mixed with the birdsong, he thinks he can hear a human voice, although distance and what could be the sound of sobbing are distorting it. He looks round, and eventually

makes out a small dark patch that seems to be moving rest-
lessly up against the asylum's whitewashed wall. As he
focusses on it, he realises the patch is a person, sometimes
standing up, sometimes crouching down. The hands are
scratching at the wall; the voice is directed upwards, but
rather than up into the evening sky, the person seems content
for it to carry over the wall and be heard on the other side.
Ariel can only hear snatches of what the man is saying, and
realises that it is the distance and the sobbing that prevent
him hearing the rest.

"Mama . . . can you hear me? I'm here . . . it's your son,
Hugo. Can you hear me, Mama? I haven't abandoned you,
I'm here, beside you . . ."

★ ★ ★

I don't want to spend the night in Gualeguay. As soon as I
get there I'm going to discover a way to leave the place, and
if that's impossible at this time of night, I'll find a car, this
or another one, someone who wouldn't mind making a few
pesos by taking me back to Buenos Aires. As we arrive in the
town I can see the bikers celebrating everywhere: they've all
got cans of beer, and one of them has taken out his guitar
and started to sing "Salamanqueando pa' m'". The kids are
parading "Granny Toyota" on their shoulders round the
main square.

I'm waiting for my driver: he's gone to tell his wife he
won't be back before tomorrow morning. I'm sitting at a
table at the rear of the Monte Carlo. Everyone else is out in
the street. No-one has asked me what I want to drink. So
much the better. I've already spent more than enough time

and money on this trip, and got nothing out of it, beyond discovering that as my father predicted, my mother came to a bad end, that Acuña must have dumped her just as she dumped us.

What I could never have dreamt is that the only one to stay with her would be my brother, the only one, the good son, the Spaniard, the *goy*, the other half.

DAYS OF 1937

THE PIANIST AT THE CAFÉ BOSTON FINISHED HIS INTER-
pretation of "Smoke Gets in Your Eyes" with the arpeggio
flourish that infallibly drew a less half-hearted applause than
usual from his late-night audience. He acknowledged the
clapping with a smile and a slight nod of the head, *urbi et orbi*.
Before closing the piano, he thrust the thumb and first finger
of his right hand into a small bowl placed on it, then raised
to his nose a pinch of the cocaine so thoughtfully offered
by the house. The *prise* — he used the French word, just like
the girls at Les Ambassadeurs — immediately seemed to
restore his flagging energy at this late hour.

It was a Monday, and almost midnight. Relegated to a
distant past were the ladies in their splendid hats who came
to take tea, talkative and enthralled by the assortment of
sandwiches and "returnable" cakes, which meant they could
hesitate over their gluttonous choice until they had eaten
them all, one by one. Gone too were the couples of the cocktail hour: women wearing less sensible hats, often with veils
that should have lent an air of mystery to their rapacious
gazes; polished men whose arch looks and brilliantine spoke
of unsurprising intentions. At that time of day they drank

"concoctions" presented on silver chrome trays, and the fantastically coloured alcoholic drinks were sipped unhurriedly; cigarette smoke that at times smelt sweet, at others more acrid, filled the air until well past nine o'clock.

For each of these very different publics, the pianist had a suitable repertoire, which he modified intuitively: he sensed instinctively when to move on from "Ramona" to "The Man I Love", knew exactly when to launch into his own much-lauded arrangement of "In a Persian Market". After ten, everything became less easy to define, both in terms of audience and conversation: voices had been known to be raised, or indiscreet words spoken in a whisper. To avoid being turned away if they came on their own (the Boston was a zealous guardian of its reputation) some women enlisted the help of a female friend, perhaps temporary but of unimpeachable behaviour, or of a *chevalier servant* who had no interest in the female gender.

This Monday there were few people in the café. The pianist did not recognise any of the faces, received no approving looks as he began a French potpourri that usually went down well: "Smoke Gets in Your Eyes" had been preceded by "J'attendrai", which merged with "Parlez-moi d'amour", followed by "Mon cœur est un violon". The cold, refreshing burst that shot up from his nose to his brain allowed him to push aside any thoughts that the audience might be unresponsive. Ivan the barman would have his usual whisky sour ready for him, and together they would discuss the contradictory, disheartening news from Europe.

But that night Ivan had been replaced – or rather, since

he was irreplaceable, it would be better to say: in his place was — a young dark-skinned boy with a soft drawl — from Corrientes perhaps, or even Paraguay? who — so the pianist thought — would not normally have been let out of the kitchen. In place of his usual cocktail, this unknown barman prepared him a "Seventh Cavalry" and could not help betraying complete ignorance about the news of the day. The pianist told himself that good manners did not mean he was obliged to talk to him, so after exchanging a few pleasantries he turned his back and took his drink to a table which although not reserved for him was usually free, due to its unfortunate position between bar and kitchen.

He was sitting there, filled with a vague sense of enthusiasm and even vaguer thoughts, when the one-night barman came over and handed him a folded piece of paper. He took it with a muttered "Thanks" and read, not without amazement: "Please, maestro, play: 'Allein in einer grossen Stadt'". He immediately looked round to see who might have made such a request; he could not have explained why he first looked for a woman on her own, whose presence there was unlikely; then he sought out a lone man, but it seemed impossible to associate the few he could see with a song like that; as for the couples in the audience, they were not paying any attention to what was going on around them. He convinced himself that the woman who had made the request (he had decided she was someone about forty years old, blonde, wistful and ironic, with Dietrich's absent gaze) must have anticipated his curiosity and momentarily left the room to avoid detection.

This conjecture, hastily invented, satisfied him. Yes, the next sip of his unwanted cocktail would be the last. No matter if he sacrificed ten minutes of his break, he would return to the piano and demonstrate his prowess with this tune that he played very occasionally without an audience in order to feel his own sadness, safe in the knowledge that no accidental listener would recognise it.

* * *

When he woke up the next morning, he quickly opened the window in his rented room as if the noise from the corner of Calle Tucumán, opposite the threatening bulk of the Law Courts, would clear away the cobwebs of sleep. The previous night's episode came back to him only half an hour later under the shower, when he caught himself humming the tune he had been asked to play. He wondered if he had not dreamt the message's neat handwriting, together with his different versions of the tune, which did not seem either to please or displease the dwindling, unenthusiastic public still waiting for some sordid miracle to happen before giving up on their day. Why had he not asked the barman to point out the person who had given him the indeterminately coloured scrap of paper? At what moment had the manager, on the till, decided it was time to close? His expressionless features, the barely perceptible jerk of his head, were the same every night; at this sign, the pianist usually went from whatever tune he was playing into "These Foolish Things", playing the final bars with a gradual *ralenti* that left the very last notes floating in mid-air, while he lifted his foot from the pedal and allowed the silence to become audible before he closed the lid of the Steinway.

No, he had not questioned the stand-in barman, and a last look at the few tables still occupied was enough to confirm that these anonymous nightbirds had little or nothing to do with all that the song suggested to him. But he had no desire to pore over his album of Berlin memories yet again. He was determined to banish any nostalgia: before abandoning the city he had played the piano during rehearsals for reviews at the Theater des Westens and the Metropol, only to be replaced three days before opening night by an orchestra not always of the same standard as the Lewis Ruth Band; he had accompanied imitators of Fritzi Massary, "*die deutsche Mistinguette*", on records they made before they became famous. He had never played as a soloist in places like the Boston or the Copper Kettle: "top-notch" places. (This description, learnt soon after he arrived in the Rio de la Plata, had already lost for him any hint of ridiculous pretension, and he used it regularly, like many other inhabitants of this city beside the unmoving river.)

But the anxiety that overwhelmed him at about nine o'clock each night, and which the administration's pharmaceutical gifts did nothing to dispel, was something he had only experienced in this city. He had fantasies about the lonely, distinguished woman whose emotions would be stirred by his piano playing, a "well-appointed" widow who might secure him a less uncertain future; the cinema director who would discover him as his saviour, the man capable of lending a touch of European class to his uncouth

45

fictions. He had eventually realised that in his position, on the periphery of this new society that was at one and the same time transparent and yet hermetically compartmentalised, he was destined to grow old without a pension or any benefits, with none of the consolations known as "social conquests" his compatriots had won thanks to the Nazis. Practical worries such as these usually called for a double dose of the comforting powder; then in place of the typical burst, it was as if a frozen butterfly took flight between his eyes, fluttering a long while in the front of his mind, helping to postpone the return to his room, his temporary neighbours and the rock-like Doña Pilar, their vigilant landlady.

He had understood at once that his housemates' profession as "dancers" was a euphemism. He had become accustomed to breakfast being a shared lunch of leftovers from previous days. He watched as "the girls" came to table: still half-asleep, and loosely wrapped in their faded dressing-gowns, with traces of the night's make-up still on their faces. The eldest often still floated in the clouds of ether she had taken hours earlier to vanquish her insomnia; some mornings the smell was so sharp that one of the younger ones would tell her to "stop abusing the bottles"; the response, with lowered gaze, was a muttered "hoofer" which, for some reason the foreign observer could never understand, was taken as an insult by the others. One day he explained to them that on Broadway they would be called "chorus girls"; a short while later he had surprised one of them using the term on the telephone, possibly to a doubtful impresario ("You are talking to a famous chorus girl"). This friendly banter with colourful

46

characters took on a different, altogether more distressing aspect whenever he imagined himself still a part of it in ten years' time.

And ten years earlier? He remembered himself as being full of expectations and plans. Among his acquaintances he was used to hearing that it was the Nazi triumph which had ruined everything, as if this were a catastrophe that had come like a bolt out of the blue, and not the all too obvious response of a world that for more than a decade those same individuals had done their best to ignore, dismiss, or push to the margins. It was they, or rather those famous friends of theirs whose reflected glory they basked in, who considered themselves to be Berlin, or Germany, or the only parts of them that mattered. Beyond their glittering circles lurked dark, excluded masses, worthy of mention only for their woeful lack of political awareness.

He had to admit that, above and beyond any historical hypothesis, the individual biological cycle obeys its own laws: he had turned forty-eight now, and his prestige had not been sufficient to accumulate the capital necessary to allow him to envisage twilight years free of want, although he was not frightened of complete ruin. It was simply the complete uncertainty, the absence of any imaginable future that some nights led him to walk down Cangallo or Viamonte, cross the Paseo de Julio, and seek out those dimly-lit, distant spots where the city faded out in bars whose sordidness was not even picturesque, or boarding houses supposedly linked to the nearby port.

This invisible port exerted its pull over him: wharves, ships barely suggested by the smell of rust that the first warm spring breezes made especially evocative. The water and the craft remained no more than phantoms, because it was impossible for him to get near them; the customs and police were suspicious of anyone strolling at night along those dark and desolate fringes of the city. But he could imagine the fleeting reflections, constantly appearing and disappearing, of the dock lights in that black water. He could hear, or believe he heard, the rhythmic, laconic slap of the water against flaking hulls, the promising murmur of engines now at rest but which at any moment could roar into life and push these floating palaces off towards Europe. He saw the Rio de la Plata, like the Atlantic Ocean it was part of, exclusively in terms of the distance that separated him from Europe; it would have been pointless to remind him that if he had travelled out in a straight line, he would have come to Cape Town: in the map of his imagination there was only one cardinal point: North-north-east.

These nocturnal wanderings, which never allowed him to attain the object of his desire, led him to spurn his friends gathered in the Viejo Luna to share a purely nostalgic *choucroute*. He also neglected the docile Inesita, whose tiny breasts were so sensitive to his touch ("*eine andere Partitur*"), and of whom he remembered above all, especially between the sheets, the perfume of wild herbs and damp meadows, but whose ability to excite him was already beginning to wane.

* * *

He received the second message almost a month after the first. Returning to the piano after a visit to the toilets, he found it folded on the polished black wood of the Steinway, and even before he opened it, recognised the colour – somewhere between pale orange and peach – of the paper. The handwriting, clear and without affectation, was exactly as he remembered it. This time the tune requested was "Frage nicht warum".

He was no less surprised than at the first message, but a coincidence prevented it having the same impact on his imagination: he had asked to finish playing at half-past eleven, because at midnight he had an important, unusual engagement. So he did no more than cast an impatient glance at the few people in the café while he played the tune which, without the voice of Richard Tauber, seemed to him unmemorable, added a few plangent chords to round it off, then closed the piano lid without adding his usual "musical finale". Fresh uncertainties were rushing through his mind, and the hasty inhalation that signalled the end of another day's work this time pierced his skull like a long sharp needle driving him on to an unknown adventure.

A taxi was waiting at the corner of Diagonal Norte. He gave him an address on Calle Parera while he took a deep, steady breath, as though trying not to waste any trace of cocaine that might still be sticking to his nostrils. For the first time he was going to play at a *souper* in the house of "upper-crust" people. In his mind, he had gone over his repertoire, dismissing tunes that might not fit in with an audience he imagined to be demanding and sophisticated, and he was still uncertain whether to start with "You and the Night and the Music" or "Orchids by Moonlight". He had written down the prestigious double-barrelled name on a piece of paper together with the address. When he arrived, he wanted to look at it once more, to make sure he knew it off by heart, and as he pulled it out of his pocket, another folded scrap of peach-coloured paper came with it, on which someone, who at that moment he did not have the time to try to imagine, had asked him to play a German song he thought had long been forgotten.

The manservant who showed him in (could he be a butler, that figure so much in demand in Argentine cinema?) took his coat and hat and immediately handed them to a maid, then led him to the piano, strategically placed between two rooms in which six or seven small tables were laid for the guests. Chatting, smiling, champagne glasses in hand, they came in through a door beyond which he could glimpse a library. Without giving it a second thought, he launched straight into "Just a Gigolo", smiling broadly as he observed the cast of characters searching for their names on tiny cards barely visible in among all the silverware, porcelain and embroidered napkins. It seemed to him they were about to put on a performance for which they all knew their roles perfectly. A tall man with a bald head and a bushy moustache gave him a brief nod by way of greeting; he decided he must be the host.

The pianist soon realised no-one was listening to him. He himself had trouble finding the right level amid the enthusiastic chorus of voices reverberating around him. When a waiter placed a glass of champagne on the piano lid, he waited timidly for several minutes before tasting it. Without neglecting the music, from his observation post he watched the different courses being served: to start with, the waiters brought in some silver platters heaped with crayfish and other seafood; the next dish appeared to be meat, or perhaps game, surrounded by chopped-up vegetables, all served with a clear sauce. Occasionally a woman's gaze met his own, and did not move on again as he expected; with a mixture of indifference and brazenness, they studied him for what he was: a meteorite dressed in a dinner jacket. It occurred to him that there might be a hint of sexual curiosity behind those looks, but he also thought it better not to have any illusions: these expensive creatures bathed in Guerlain could only brush up against him fleetingly, absent-mindedly, and only with their eyes.

"Do you play tangos too?"

The question startled him. The woman who had spoken the words over his shoulder was mature in years, slim as a pencil, and smiled without fear of revealing her protruding teeth. Between the thumb and middle finger of her right hand, she was nervously brandishing a cigarette holder. Before he could reply, she insisted:

"Do you know 'La muchacha del circo'?"

He smiled in acknowledgement, and launched into the tune which, like so many other tangos, he could play by ear but had never included in his repertoire.

"Wait, don't be in such a hurry."

The woman turned to the guests, who at that moment were slowly finishing a *bavarois*, and instructed them:

"Listen to La Quiroga."

After two false starts, he found the key to accompany her. Pleased, he discovered he could follow the tune without any false notes, and was able to anticipate or emphasise the parodic effects, the lisping, or the hoarse drawl of her imitation. When she finished, the applause that greeted her seemed sincere if excessive, almost without irony.

"Go on, now do La Lamarque!"

Under cover of the general merriment, several of the guests had slipped from their tables to join the few who had already left the dinner and congregated in the library, cups of coffee in hand. The woman seemed to be enjoying herself rather more than her rapidly dwindling audience.

"Don't be so rude, listen to the one and only, the great Mercedes Simone . . ."

She ordered him to play "Cantando". It did not take him long to realise that this time it was no parody. She might lack the unerring spontaneous musicality of her model, but it was obvious the emotions were truly felt as she gave herself to the song.

I was born to sing,
I've lived my life singing,
And as I don't know how to cry
It's singing I shall die.

This time the applause was less enthusiastic, briefer. Everyone was answering the silent call from the next room, and in a few minutes all the tables were deserted.

"Well, it seems to me an artist should know when it's time

for her to leave the stage," the woman said to ripples of laughter, and waved her cigarette holder with a dramatic flourish. "Thanks, maestro."

That word "maestro" jolted him. He was accustomed to hearing it as a polite compliment, not often used, but devoid of irony; now, in the voice of this woman walking away from him without a backward glance, this woman who seemed to talk in inverted commas as if constantly laughing at herself, the word reminded him that he had read it in those anonymous requests at the café: it was like a quotation from a text whose meaning he could not grasp.

The same discreet manservant who had ushered him in came over to hand him an envelope. There was no need for him to open it to recognise the crisp weight of a wad of banknotes.

"This way, please."

He followed the man, casting a last look back at the exuberant table bouquets, with their unexpected combination of flowers. In two portraits that looked like Winterhalter copies, he recognised first of all the features of the man (with a fuller head of hair) whose nod of greeting had suggested he was the evening's host, and then the slender woman with the perpetually mocking smile, in which the painter had carefully concealed her buck teeth.

The servant led him to the kitchen parlour. Waiting for him on a card table covered with a plain tablecloth he found a selection of the food he had seen being served in the dining-rooms; to one side, a bottle of wine had replaced the champagne. He told himself it would be more dignified to leave without trying these undoubted delicacies, but curiosity and the sudden flashing vision of Doña Pilar's stews did away with all thoughts of pride. He poured himself a glass, and was able to verify that this wine was far superior to anything he was used to drinking.

"Is the lady who sang the mistress of the house?" he plucked up the courage to ask a moment later. Only two maids were still in the kitchen, doing the washing-up. They looked enquiringly at each other before the elder of the two replied with a curt "yes" and left the room. The younger one came over to him, and spoke in a low, rapid voice.

"The master doesn't like her to do her impressions, but when she's had a bit to drink no-one can stop her. They say that before she married him, she used to sing in the . . ."

The return of her companion carrying a tray full of precariously perched dirty plates and cutlery cut short her confidences. On her heels came the manservant, almost hidden behind a huge arrangement of irises and lilies. When he saw the pianist had finished eating and drinking, he asked him if he would like a coffee, in a tone which suggested the visit was at an end. The pianist said a vague "good night" to no-one in particular. His coat and hat were now waiting for him by the service exit.

When he opened the street door, he took a deep breath. He searched in his pocket for the peach-coloured piece of paper and read once more: "Please, maestro, play: 'Frage nicht warum'". But his thoughts were racing in another direction, so he pushed aside any supposition his imagination might make as to who could have sent him the request. He walked back to his rented room. In the silent, empty streets he felt as if he was awakening from a dream that had confused him with a whirl of images and sensations. Without much hope of finding any remaining consolation, he breathed in as hard as he could, but the only cold sensation that rushed up his nose was from the chill night air.

* * *

Often over the next few months he imagined a third message. By tradition, destiny knocked three times: three wishes, three blows of the cane to signal the start of a play at the theatre. Then one afternoon, when he lifted the lid of the Steinway, he found a folded sheet of peach-coloured paper which had obviously been just thin enough to slip through the gap when the piano was closed. He unfolded it with nervous expectation, but found there was nothing written there; he turned the sheet over but could not find so much as a word or a scribble on the paper. He thrust it into his pocket without a further thought, and that afternoon began his recital with "Es gibt nur einmal", a Viennese march whose imperial nostalgia had always irritated him; irrationally, this was his way of responding to whoever had left the blank piece of paper. The evening passed with no sign of the wretched prankster coming forward: he decided it must have been someone from Vienna laughing at him as a Berlin emigré . . .

He was in the midst of a Latin potpourri, between "Frenesi'" and "Perfidia", when he noticed the arrival of the deputy director of Radio Belgrano, who had been introduced to him some months earlier. He smiled warmly and nodded, and the newcomer returned the compliment. He was

55

accompanied by a very young woman with chestnut hair and a translucent skin. During his break, he accepted the invitation to sit with them, and kissed the unknown woman's hand. He knew that this gesture, so unusual in this part of the world, gave him a certain prestigious aura, which he had once heard described as that of a "European beau". This time however, the recipient stared back at him without smiling; the expression he could read in her face was not one of pleasure but rather of suspicion. From the few minutes he spent at the table, the impression he got was of a silent, perhaps shy young girl, whose eyes occasionally shone with a glint that suggested a mixture of ambition and spite.

He had become so accustomed to being kept waiting and being put off that he had to contain his amazement at the proposal made by this acquaintance of his, who had no reason to make him any friendly gesture: to play as a soloist, every Monday at 11 p.m. in a programme whose provisional title was "Nostalgia for Europe". He saw no point in concealing his enthusiasm. At this early hour, the welcoming bowl had not yet made its appearance on the piano; his spontaneous reaction had none of the exaggerated emphasis the chemicals brought out in him. He thanked them for the opportunity they were offering him "to reach a wider public" with his repertoire. The deputy director of the popular radio station explained that his pieces would be framed by readings ("romantic, picturesque, moving evocations of the great European cities") presented by the young actress accompanying him.

"Someone to watch," the radio director told him next day

in his office. "Magaldi met her during a tour and brought her to Buenos Aires . . . She wasn't exactly a success in the theatre, but Chas de Cruz has offered her a small part in a film he's going to make with Quartucci. And we'll see what she's like on radio . . ."

The contract he was proffered, and which he quickly signed, was for one month only. This would at least allow him to repay money he had borrowed from friends, partially renew his wardrobe, and to allay Doña Pilar's suspicions. Beyond these modest aims, all he could hope was that the sponsors would be pleased with his performance and extend his contract. But it did not take him long to realise that his music was of only secondary importance in this production: the idea was above all to give "an opportunity" to this girl who seemed rebellious and yet compliant, whose strong character seemed to him only barely concealed. Away from the microphone, she had a freshness unspoilt by childhood hardships and humiliations; in front of the terrible metal object she lost all her natural qualities and, completely disoriented, poured out endless quantities of mawkish bad taste.

He got used to there being a car waiting for her at midnight when they left the radio station. One Monday night, however, he could not see the black shiny limousine parked a few yards from the door, so he made so bold as to ask if he could wait with her.

"I'm not waiting," was her curt reply; and then as if to correct any impression this might give of harshness, she added with a forced laugh: "There won't be any more chauffeur-driven cars for me."

He invited her to have something to eat ("if it doesn't seem too cheap for you") at the restaurant, which he modestly referred to as a "bar", where he spent the evenings when not playing at the Boston. She gladly accepted.

"When I first came to Buenos Aires I couldn't even afford a bar like this," she said, imitating the way he pronounced "bar".

They both laughed, and for the first time there was a relaxed and carefree atmosphere between them. He imagined that the sentimental, and doubtless professional setback signified by the car's absence had led her to abandon, at least for a few hours, the cautious diffidence she usually adopted in her relationships with men.

They were finishing the bottle of wine when her question took him aback:

"What are you going to do when the programme finishes?"

He in turn asked her if she was sure the programme would not continue. For what seemed to him like an endless moment, she stared at him with a look of weary certainty.

"At the end of the month, it's over. That's all there is to it."

He did not wish to ask her why she was so sure, but surmised that the lack of the limousine and its uniformed chauffeur were the explanation.

"You play the piano with a lot of feeling." She was changing the topic of conversation, and her tone of voice seemed sincere and unaffected. "That's obvious. But — how shall I put it? — your music isn't for everyone . . . I don't mean it's only for foreigners like you, but . . . Well, I wouldn't like to see you in a tight spot, at your age . . ."

Scarcely able to believe his ears, he understood that this child, who had aroused his sense of compassion, felt sorry for *him*. Furthermore: that the thirty years between them, which he had become used to ignoring, were plainly the chief source of her concern. Together with the contradictory feelings that he tried in vain to control, he felt the electric shock of the need for the kind of chemical boost that on other evenings was at his fingertips in the Boston. He realised he could no longer play the role, however unconvincing, of the man of the world consoling an unfortunate beginner. This particular beginner was sufficiently clear-sighted and level-headed to have seen through the character he thought he was representing. He felt he ought to say something, anything. After a great deal of effort, he managed a smile, which must have seemed bitter, but he no longer cared about keeping up the pretence. He heard himself say:

"I don't know, perhaps I'll go back to Germany . . ."

* * *

On the 22nd of July 1937, the German-registered liner *Gonzenheim* sailed from Dock C in Buenos Aires, bound for Bremen. On the third-class passenger list appeared the name "Jürgen Rütting, profession: musician."

In some mythologies, death is not a sudden event, the abrupt transition from one instant when there is life to another when it no longer exists. Instead, it is represented by a symbolic journey, which can be understood as a process of letting go and of learning at the same time.

It is possible to imagine that during this transition there subsist, like islands floating in a night-time sea, fragments of awareness, memories, voices and images, remnants of the gradually dimming existence, temporary baggage the traveller clings onto for a brief but imprecise length of time that our instruments cannot register.

Nothing entitles us to believe in the persistence on those islands of the moments which the wayfarer may have thought decisive in his life. Perhaps all that clings to them is flotsam from a shipwreck. It would be useless to expect that these scraps, which crumble even as we name them, could provide us with a portrait of the person crossing the divide. Perhaps it is only precisely as shards that they can catch the attention of any improbable observer who stumbles across them: their condition as brief fragments of a truncated story, the random pieces of a jigsaw that will never now be completed.

VIEW OF DAWN OVER A LAKE

THE WOMAN OPENED THE DOOR AS STEALTHILY AS SHE HAD shut the one to her own room and had walked first along a corridor and then a flight of stairs that were also lit by the dim night-light.

She entered the room cautiously. It was not similar to hers, but the ante-room of a suite. Through an arch she could make out a small sitting-room, with no sign of anything personal in it; a half-open door acted as a screen to the room where the patient must be sleeping. She hesitated, then gently pushed it open.

A grey, pulsating light lit up the bed where the emaciated body lay. The glow came from a television set that was switched on with the sound off. A mass of cables and tubes linked the body to bags suspended from a drip trolley, doling out drop by drop the substances that sought to prolong a fragile life; in among all this tangle, the woman did not at first notice the earphones the patient was wearing, with their invisible wires.

On the television screen, heavily made-up figures were gesticulating against a backdrop of mist that seemed to be rising from the surface of a lake. The woman looked for the patient's eyes. Deep in darkened sockets, almost entirely covered by the wrinkled membranes that had once been eyelids, they were not closed. They were staring at the television devoid of all expression.

The woman edged forward to a chair. The patient did not seem aware of her presence. A long moment's silence passed before he spoke, in a surprisingly firm voice.

"Are you the new nurse?"

The woman said nothing. She looked at the screen, on which possibly mythological monsters kept appearing and disappearing in the mist that swirled around the bejewelled figures, their features emphasised by operatic make-up. She realised they must be singers, and that words and music were justifying what to her looked like a grotesque pantomime. Another lengthy pause went by before the patient asked:

"Do I know you?"

At that instant, their eyes met for the first time. She did not reply at once. When she did, her voice, weaker than the patient's, was that of someone groping for words with great difficulty.

"I don't know. Perhaps. Marcia, Enrique, Marcos, Mercedes, Clara . . . Do any of those names mean anything to you?"

The patient's gaze returned to the silent screen. He took some time before replying with another question.

"Why are you speaking to me in Spanish?"

She smiled faintly: she had not realised that until now the man had been talking in French.

"Because I know you understand it. Because you used to

62

speak it. Twenty-five years ago, in Buenos Aires."

A laugh, immediately cancelled out by a coughing fit, shook the patient's body.

"And who was I twenty-five years ago?"

An awkward silence followed. They had spoken, some kind of contact had been made, and now the silence could only mean they did not want to say any more. Both of them sought refuge in the spectacle of the characters weighed down with paste jewels, fatuously moving their lips on the silent screen.

After a while, the woman felt that the patient's eyes were no longer staring at the television, but at her. She stared back at him, amazed at the harshness and intensity those weary eyes could summon up, like the shockingly firm voice in a body that was no more than an empty shell.

"Have you come here from Argentina?"

"No, I've lived in Geneva for years."

"So now all of a sudden you think you see in me . . . who exactly? A long-lost love?"

She sighed before responding.

"It's not as simple as that. You never allow anyone to photograph you. And I've read you get a new face every three years."

"I'm very lucky. I know how to forget. With every new face, my memory is wiped clean. You should try it some-time."

The words sounded self-assured, but the voice behind them was flat, expressionless. He went on:

"Where did you read about me? I'm a rich person, but not

well known, almost anonymous. Nobody interviews me, nobody takes the trouble to write about me."

The woman could not hide a certain satisfaction.

"I paid a private investigation agency to find out who was behind a production of Handel's *Alcina* performed on the lake at Constanza."

This did not seem to impress the patient.

"And did you find out anything worth the money you paid?"

"I'm not sure. Possibly. That Señor Ronald Duparc was naturalised as a Swiss citizen after only five years' residence in the canton of Vaud, instead of the ten stipulated in the Confederation's laws. That when he arrived here in 1977, he was carrying a Panamanian passport. That banking secrecy prevents anyone knowing the amounts he deposited in the Union des Banques Suisses and in the Crédit Suisse. That two years ago, under another pseudonym, he set up a foundation to produce opera festivals, the first of which is to be held this summer."

The patient did not answer immediately. He seemed to be waiting for further information, which was not forthcoming.

"Is that all?"

"That was enough. The banking secrets, the false names, the identity documents purchased, may not be sufficient. People usually give the game away through details they see as unimportant, or seem too private to betray a face that has vanished after all the operations."

"And that face belonged to someone you knew, someone you were searching for . . ."

"I wasn't searching for it. I thought I had forgotten it. I knew that person, or thought I knew him, at a time when I was someone else too."

She smiled bleakly and went on:

"I didn't need surgeons. The years did the work themselves."

Once again, the patient waited for words that did not come. He insisted:

"And I suppose you have something serious against that person."

"I don't know how to explain it. I'd managed to forget him. Many years ago I could have given you a precise answer. Something like: to have disappeared with a kidnap ransom that he was supposed to hand over to a group of . . . dreamers; to find out that the person kidnapped was his accomplice, and that they had planned all along to share the ransom paid by a multinational company between them. But none of that matters any more. Perhaps I hated him because he had shown he was not a dreamer like us. And now, when at last I am face to face with him, I want to hate him because I hated him in my youth, and to hate him now makes me feel young again."

When the patient spoke again, his voice had lost some of the impersonal sonorousness of a radio presenter.

"You talk of yourself as though you were a character in a novel. I wouldn't be surprised if you invented novels around yourself with real people in them. Like me, for example."

"That's possible. But I put my trust in chance. In addition to his ideological outbursts, which at the time seemed sincere to us, the character I knew all that time ago had a passion

— if not secret, at least a private one. One enthusiastic night of celebration, he let something slip. He talked about an opera, or more exactly about his dream of putting on what was then an almost forgotten opera, not on a stage but in the midst of nature, on an island or beside a lake. Two months ago, when I saw a poster for a summer festival and recognised the title of the opera and the name of the composer, I remembered the old dream lodged who knows where in the depths of my memory."

"That's absurd. An opera-loving political militant?"

"I never used the word 'militant'."

"It's implicit in everything you've said, in your nostalgia, your disenchantment, your stubborn blindness. And now you want me to be that traitor. Why? To kill me? Do you really think you can get your youth back by killing me?"

"The agency told me when you would be in the clinic. I chose this place so I could get near you. I don't know if I was thinking of killing you."

"You're living a melodrama which fits in with your vision of the world. Unfortunately, real life tends to be more ironic. I lead people to believe I am in here for my umpteenth facial surgery. In fact, I am dying, of a perfectly ordinary cancer."

He paused a second before adding:

"Here too, like all your kind, you arrive too late, you get it all wrong, and you leave no trace in the real world."

Once again, his laughter brought on a fit of coughing that racked his body. She watched him writhing in the bed, not showing the slightest concern.

"Killing you would not settle any old score: if it ever

66

existed, it's long forgotten. But I always wanted to kill. If I've never done so, it was simply to avoid going to jail. But now I feel there's little purpose left to continue in what this world has become. Perhaps it's the moment to allow myself this luxury."

"Without an alibi? Aren't you trying to give birth to the new man, or a more just society, or whatever other excuse you can find to kill with a clean conscience? I admire your courage. I don't think you have any children, or like many other women, had children who they encouraged to take up arms on their behalf, children whose death now gives them a certain journalistic notoriety . . . You are courageous enough to accept your own hatred, your desire to kill, without any emotional alibi. I admire you."

With a surprisingly forceful gesture, the patient tore off his earphones and pressed a button on the remote control. The music and singing reduced them to silence.

Verdi prati, selve amene,
Perderete la beltà

"Money used to buy arms can also be used for this," he declared. "I told you, you've arrived too late. You would be killing a dying man, a discreet patron of the arts, someone with no relation to those ancient stories that are of no interest to anyone any more."

He laughed, or coughed, once more.

"God got here before you."

The woman sat for a moment without moving. When she

stood up, it was as though she were weighed down by an immense weariness. She walked towards the door of the room, but suddenly halted, as if struck by an afterthought.

"But . . . I never believed in God . . ."

Unhurriedly, but precisely and without hesitation, she disconnected all the tubes and cables connecting the patient to his sources of survival. The man did not react as he watched her at work. She could spot no fear or hatred in his mineral eyes. She stood for a few minutes staring at him, as if expecting some signal that his life had ebbed away, but there was no grimace or rattle that announced his end. Eventually she stretched out two fingers and closed the icy eyelids on two eyes that challenged her sightlessly.

Back in her own room, she opened the French windows that led out onto her narrow balcony. Day was dawning. A cool breeze heralded a summer morning, carrying with it the scent of lime trees and honeysuckle. She took a deep breath. For the first time in months, perhaps years, she felt at peace with herself. She buttoned up the coat she had put on over her nightdress and stood watching the slow dawn. Through the mist over the lake she saw a silent rower pass by. She heard the cries of ducks and seagulls. Her mind was filled with images and voices from childhood, a past which had not revisited her in a long, long time. Her memories brought no sadness or unwelcome revelations. She surrendered to them, as though sinking into a warm lap, where she at last might find some rest.

BUDAPEST

THE DRIVER WAITING AT THE AIRPORT SHOT A QUICK GLANCE at the address on the card David Lerman held out, unable to pronounce the words. His only question was whether David wanted to drive through the city or round it. He preferred to travel through it. The second question was if he wanted to go alongside the Danube or across Heroes' Square. This time David chose the second alternative. "*Schön!*" the driver approved with a smile. Using the rudimentary German the two men managed to communicate in, he explained it was longer, and perhaps less picturesque, but far more interesting that way.

The driver could not have been more than thirty, but he conjured up episodes from before his time as though he had been an adult witness to them — a knack he must have inherited together with the tales his parents told him. David felt no wish to tell him his mother was a native of this city, and had left it in 1938, when her parents took her to Argentina, where she was to marry and give birth to David. Instead, he sat back and surveyed the urban landscape, palely lit by an invisible February sun, filtering it through these superimposed images: a palimpsest on which, like X-rays, his memory took him back to his mother's recollections of a distant childhood, while at the same time his driver recounted the more recent turbulent history of every street and square they passed through.

"Over there! On the left, behind the columns! That's where the giant statue of Stalin was. They pulled it down in the '56 uprising. Then, when the Soviet tanks rolled in, in spite of the repression no-one dared put the little father of all peoples back . . . Stalin in Heroes' Square! That was just too much . . ."

David meanwhile was concentrating on the pompous Habsburg architecture of the Széchenyi Baths his mother had frequented as a child, playing in the swimming pools with their artificial waves. Or had that been on Margit island? She also told stories about another pool where golden lights and mechanically produced bubbles tried to give the impression you were bathing in champagne . . . David recalled having read that a lot of the greatest Hollywood directors and producers were from Hungary. It seemed to him only natural they should have grown up in this land once so full of decorative invention, that would help fiction infiltrate reality.

The car was advancing slowly along the Andrassy út (which had once been called Stalin Avenue and Avenue of the People's Republic, although no-one had ever used those names). The façades had not been cleaned or restored, but still boasted the bullet holes from October 1956. A mutilated balcony, or fragments of polychrome majolica in the Kodaly körut or in Oktogon, seemed to David eloquent lessons as to the virtue of accepting the scars of the past rather than effacing them by skin-deep surgery of the kind the already distant German "miracle" had imposed.

The driver managed to reach a bridge and cross the Danube without passing any of the international hotels whose gigantic steel and glass forms had erupted over the past decade like hideous boils. Yet on the Teréz út David thought he saw a McDonald's in an art nouveau pavilion next to a railway station.

"It used to be the West station buffet," the irrepressible driver told him. "It was in ruins and there was no money to rebuild it. The city leased it to McDonald's but insisted they leave it in its original state."

Apart from the huge illuminated yellow letter M, thought David. But he knew better than to say this out loud. As they crossed the river, he peered down at the wharves, slumbering among traces of snow, at the silhouettes of bare trees etched in black and white, and also kept to himself the memory (where was it he had read it?) of the Jews mown down at the water's edge so that their corpses would be swept away by the river current. Was that at the end of 1944? He told himself that he too was a storehouse of other people's stories, stories the driver may have been unaware of, or had relegated to the blurred margins of a past in which he had no interest.

By now they were climbing the heights of Buda. Beyond the fortress, not just Pest, but the whole city was spread out before David like an architect's model, a stage set dotted with invented gardens, palaces, and bridges that did not correspond to any precise historical period, but once again reminded him of the hidden genealogy that linked this city to Hollywood.

★ ★ ★

Three weeks earlier, in his *atelier* in Clamart, he had received one of the periodic visits from J.-M. Henriot, whose ostensible line of business was running an art gallery in Neuchâtel, owned by a Sirio-Colombian firm.

At first the visit had been like all the previous ones: the loud greeting at the door, the theatrical embrace, followed by a swift move into the kitchen for the bottle of cognac and the glass the visitor knew exactly where to find. After which, J.-M. was accustomed to collapsing into an armchair and, in no particular order, pouring himself a generous drink, reaching into his inside pocket and, like a magician, producing an envelope which he tossed at David's feet. It was also customary for David not to bend down and pick it up in front of his visitor: he left that till later, when he was alone again. He rarely had any reason for complaint: the counterfoil for the deposit in a Swiss bank was invariably for the agreed amount.

Next, J.-M. would ask him how his work was getting on: the copy of an original in transit – the original to remain in Switzerland, the copy to be returned to the owner. (David could not help smiling as he remembered the first time he had heard of this kind of subterfuge: it was typical of a certain patron of the literary left in the Rio de la Plata, whose entire collection of Figari had been put together in this way). For years now, David had not painted pictures of his own . . . One day, he thought he had glimpsed in the gaze of his characters, his painted creatures, a mistrust and fear he had not seen in the models posing for him. The ambiguous distance, so beloved of Henry James, that art introduces between reality and its representation, in his case only seemed to add this look of suspicion, and it made his portraits unbearable by infecting them with a silent, solitary unease: his own.

This realisation, which would have pleased lesser artists, wounded David, and robbed him of the courage needed to use this difference as his own personal signature, his style. Instead, he painted only copies, believing in this way he was escaping his dilemma, and this in turn led him to forgery. His own painting had never provided him with the sums of money he could now earn for fake Utrillos, Vlamincks, or Van Dongens. It was true his talent was a minor one, but in this area he was beyond compare. Perhaps because of the disdain he felt for those who paid money for his work, he took an inordinate amount of trouble over these counterfeits. In his *atelier*, surrounded by a huge number of canvases turned against the wall, a single painting confronted the visitor: the portrait of a young woman. J.-M. had never succeeded in finding out who she was, but it was obviously this canvas that led him to ask each time he came: "So when are you going to start exhibiting again?" – a question David took less as a compliment than as a hint this might be something else he could exploit.

But that afternoon, after a quick inspection of the land-scape that David had been laying out on a canvas, following the lines and colours projected by a slide (a copy he calcu-lated he would complete satisfactorily in a few more weeks), J.-M. had said unexpectedly:

"How do you fancy a trip to Budapest?"

Seeing David's surprised look, he went on:

"It's simple. You have to go and inspect a Friedrich."

He went on to give a hasty version of a story that briefly was as follows: not far from Budapest, a countess had managed to keep a Friedrich hidden in a barn through all the fifty years of communism.

During that half century, the house, like all those which on the death of the owner were destined to pass into the hands of the state, gradually fell into a state of disrepair that was more sordid than picturesque. But History, despite the legislative urge of those who seek to explain it, is not averse to its portion of chance: the collectivist regime crumbled before the countess' health did, so that now, at the age of eighty-three, she found herself once more the undisputed owner of all her possessions. Unfortunately, she also had to cope with hugely increased taxes, and the impossible task of paying for even a limited upkeep of her property.

One of her few surviving relatives advised her to entrust the sale of furniture, tapestries and the odd painting by some minor Central European master to galleries in Munich and Zurich. At first, she had refused to part with her Friedrich, but now that there seemed no escape from her dreadful economic predicament, she decided she could not rely on her usual intermediaries. The canvas had passed through the hands of a Red Army general, who had "liberated" it from a German castle, but had neglected to include it in the inventory he had drawn up for the Moscow Academy of Fine Arts. (There were various hypotheses concerning this omission:

74

the most extraordinary being the suggestion that the general had formed a private collection for his own pleasure, the most realistic being that he had assembled a private collection which, unbeknown to the Soviet authorities, was intended to guarantee him ready money for the trips he was already planning in the capitalist world, or which might even – in a future as yet unforeseeable in the Soviet Union – help set him up permanently in the other half of the world.)

Had he entrusted the Friedrich to the countess in order to keep it safe from rival claims or expropriations? The fact is that once it had been included in the lists of Second World War "missing works of art", it was impossible to sell the painting publicly. And it was precisely in cases of this kind that J.-M.'s experience could prove invaluable. David's mission would simply be to visit the countess, verify to his own satisfaction that the painting was authentic, and inspire sufficient confidence in the old lady for her to entrust his Neuchâtel gallery with its private sale. David knew what would happen after that: once in Switzerland, the canvas would be examined by "the most eminent and trustworthy" experts. They would declare it to be merely a period copy, and then, thanks to his own expertise, the original would be kept, while a copy would be returned to Hungary in place of the original, to bring solace to the countess in her twilight years.

David had accepted on the spot.

That night, sitting facing the portrait whose identity he kept as his secret, he wondered whether he had agreed so readily to cut short the unbearable J.-M.'s visit because he wanted to enrich his experience by descending to a still deeper level of baseness (though Dostoevsky was not one of his favourite authors), or out of a sudden curiosity to visit the city in which his mother had been born.

As usual, the portrait gazed back at him inscrutably. Changeable as the weather, its eyes went from irony to scorn, from pity to fear. David knew these emotions were fictions he invented from the folds of a frown or a line at the corner of the mouth, but he never tired of playing this game, and constantly questioned his creature in search of an ever-elusive revelation.

More often than not, he fell asleep in front of the canvas.

* * *

There was no mistaking the Friedrich: the figure of a man, back to the viewer, draped in a black frock coat, hair tousled by a wind that bent trees and whipped up waves on a river, against a background of cliffs and a lowering sky. And yet this tumultous landscape transmitted a consoling silence, a strange serenity, as though by depicting the scene on canvas, the act of painting had conferred on it a calming sense of distance, of passion recollected in tranquillity.

The countess stood apart from David, watching him study the painting. David recognised her controlled anxiety, her mistrust, from the portraits he himself had painted; he even wondered whether if he took her as his subject the usual process would be inverted, and the old woman's face might lose this expression and take on an unsuspected candour instead. Her mahogany hair was badly dyed: some strands of white gave the game away. A black dress and the absence of any jewellery served to emphasise the dense network of fine wrinkles covering her face. There was not an ounce of spare flesh to mar the splendid bone structure. Her bright, wary eyes were those of a young bird of prey.

They were standing in a large drawing-room whose windows looked out onto a straggling garden. The winter afternoon light was not enough to view the painting properly, but David preferred this feeble illumination to that of the few lamps he could see, which he was sure would give off a yellow glow.

"You can unhook it and take it over to the window," the countess suggested, more as an order than as an attempt to help. Her French sounded like that of a character invented by another countess: the Countess of Ségur.

David obeyed. Over the years, the patina had deposited several layers on the original colours that would be hard for him to imitate; he would need to invent a recent cleaning to explain their absence. But it was not professional considerations that came flocking to his mind. The silence was so perfect, the dust on the few pieces of furniture lay so still, that his mind was filled with images of this woman, with no family or servants, all alone in these vast spaces that had once been imposing, if not welcoming. How did she spend her time? She did not look like someone given to nostalgia.

"It's the picture that was in the Duke of Erfurt's castle until 1945," he said, returning to the reason for his visit. "After that, all trace of it was lost."

"'All trace of it was lost' . . . you sound like an auctioneer," the countess said, with a laugh like hailstones. "I suppose that even though you will not make them public, you need some details."

David felt weary, unwilling to play his allotted role.

"You don't have to tell me anything if you don't want to. I can sense that this Friedrich means something, perhaps a lot, to you. I sense you don't want to sell it."

"Now you're talking like a child. Did you never learn that to discover you have to do something you didn't want to is what it means to be adult? Isn't that how it's always been, whatever the government?"

David hung the painting back on the wall. Away from the window, the darkness swallowed up its blues, greys, and browns. He heard himself say, as if his voice did not belong to him:

"Don't sell it. There are museums that would offer you a lot of money if you bequeathed it to them. I could put you in touch with them, or with private collectors who would accept the same conditions. But don't part with it."

The countess said nothing. A fresh light appeared in her eyes, a spark of curiosity that softened their harshness. After a few moments, she spoke.

"You're not the person I expected."

"Perhaps I'm not the person they sent to see you . . ."

The weariness he had felt only a short while before had suddenly vanished. Like a patient who discovers his diagnosis does not mention the illness of which he had been so afraid, David felt a burst of almost-forgotten energy.

★ ★ ★

Half an hour later, with the last daylight filtering into the room, he watched the countess' aquiline profile slowly fading in the darkness. The old woman's broken, harsh voice had told him (though he was not entirely sure she had been speaking to him, despite there being only the two of them in the room) about a young girl playing on her own in a castle near Erfurt, in a room where this painting had always disturbed her. More than once, she had clambered onto a chair and struggled to lift the picture from the wall to try to discover the face of the man who always had his back to her; all she was ever rewarded with was a black, grimy outline. A few years later she found out that she and her mother lived in an apartment in the castle, but were forbidden to use the main rooms and the grand entrance: the title she would one day inherit was the fruit — no doubt legitimate — of a morganatic marriage. "But these days no-one is interested in gossip from the Gotha Almanach." Many years and a war later, by now living in the house she was to grow old in, she had been sitting down with the servants to eat turnip and cabbage soup from the then thriving garden, when a roar of engines distracted them: several Red Army vehicles had pulled up outside, beyond the railings. A polite general explained to her in correct German that "the palace" had been requisitioned to billet his troops.

A brief conversation had been enough — "the general was a bit of a snob, my title impressed him, and in those days I was young and perhaps beautiful"— for the troops to be sent to look elsewhere, and for the general to stay to eat with the countess. The servants went on with their soup in the kitchen, while the house-owner and her guest, in the very same room where David was now listening to the story, opened two tins of caviar the general had produced from a briefcase bearing a military crest; the fresh bread, which had been part of the stock impounded in the city by his subordinates, had to her tasted far more delicious than any recollection of distant gastronomic treats. "Since there is no such thing as chance," it turned out that this "so presentable" Soviet officer had studied art history and had been instructed by the Moscow Fine Arts Academy to draw up a list of "available" works of art in the occupied territories.

"The rest is of no interest. Years later, the general was the military attaché in some South American republic or other when he 'chose freedom', as the expression had it in those days. His private collection found its way to Zurich. This Friedrich never appeared on his list of treasures: it had been here since 1947. It wasn't hard for me to convince him."

David stood up. As he was saying goodbye, he kissed the countess' hand, and murmured to her:

"That painting should stay here for the rest of your life. And beyond that too – in a Central European museum, for example. Please don't let it end up in the United States or Japan . . ."

He repeated his promise to put her in touch with the right people, and thought he saw a sceptical, almost encouraging smile on her by now inscrutable features.

David was still full of his new-found sense of youthful expectancy as the car drove back across the city towards the airport. Despite the darkness and the pulsating neon lights it was still only five o'clock, and he thought it might be possible to get the 7 p.m. Paris flight. At some point in the journey he told the by now tired and silent driver to pull up. He thought he had seen a particular word on a neon sign, and wanted to see whether he had dreamt it or not. The car turned down a side street and returned to the spot David had indicated. After a moment's disbelief, David got out, and without saying a word went in through a wide doorway flanked by two sooty Atlases and disappeared beneath a word whose red letters flashed on and off: *Bailongo*.

★ ★ ★

As if his entrance were like the three knocks that traditionally signal the start of a play, David just had time to make out the cramped dimensions and worn-out décor of the room before the lights dimmed and several spotlights came on, projected onto a mirrorball. Perhaps set in motion by these narrow beams of light, the globe started to rotate, and its fleeting, aquatic reflections in turn brought a number of couples out from the wings of this hidden theatre; the dance-floor was soon full. An occasional stray reflection even reached the farthest corners, where the shy and the proud, the lonely and the violent, were waiting their turn. David decided to postpone all the questions crowding into his mind, and pushed forward until he could lean at the zinc bar. Beneath a shock of brilliantined hair, the barman smiled at him. In the bar mirror, multiplied beyond belief, he could make out faded labels on the bottles: Legui rum, Old Smuggler's whisky. Before he could invent an explanation, or understand that there wasn't one, the music — a sort of foxtrot in the Harry Roy style — died away, and the couples were left standing, waiting for the next tune.

They did not have to wait long. As soon as David recognised the opening bars of "Los Mareados" by Atilio Stampone and his orchestra, without the slightest sense of incredulity or any wish to find answers, he surrendered to whatever the night might have in store. It did not surprise him in the least to see the figure of a young woman coming towards him against the light. When she was in his arms, the other couples gave way on the floor, and the two of them started to dance in silence. In her youthful face, David could not find any of the painful expressions he was always seeing — found it impossible not to see — in the posthumous portrait he had painted from memory so many years earlier. He pulled her against him and could feel her nipples tautening beneath her black dress; he pressed up against her so that she could feel the urgency of his desire. Perhaps the music would never end, perhaps she would stay in his arms all night long.

* * *

No French newspaper thought it worth reporting. Only the Buenos Aires magazine *El Cachafaz* devoted a few lines to it. Beneath a sensationalist title ("Last Tango in Budapest for the Phantom Painter") the article told of the death of David Lerman: "private sources" had apparently informed them that this occurred in a nightclub in the Hungarian capital ("he was struck down by a heart attack while in the arms of a hostess"). It reminded the reader that Lerman had been an important member of the 1960s "new figurative" movement in Argentina, that he had not had a show for many years, and that he lived in France at an unknown address.

CHRISTMAS '54

THE MAN OF LETTERS PAUSED TO LOOK UP AT THE GIGANTIC new portraits of the president and his late wife. They had been placed on either side of the vast noticeboard whose whirring letters and numbers announced the platforms for the suburban trains. These illustrious, benevolent effigies presided over the station's drowsy animation. For his photographic epiphanies, the president had long since discarded the military uniform that had brought him to power; even the morning suit, briefly favoured for images of official receptions and gala functions, had been stored away; the unremarkable suit and tie he was now pictured in showed him to be just another citizen doing his job, like all the office workers and low-ranking civil servants scurrying beneath his imposing image. As befitted a deceased person still assiduously flattered, his wife's lips and gaze hinted at a frank, open smile. She was free at last of the weight of gold and fur stoles that she had once foolishly shown off to the lens of a foreign reporter.

These presences aroused neither devotion nor revulsion in the man of letters. The reason for his indifference lay not so much in the fact that he was a foreigner or in the political scepticism which made his daily existence precarious, but in the sense of curiosity he felt for nearly every aspect of life in this paradoxical country where he had chosen to seek exile and which he could not make up his mind to leave. The Second World War had left *his* Vienna impoverished, disorientated, divided between four supposedly victorious armies. Those old friends of his who had not emigrated lived on in the crannies of a new world whose rules they dimly grasped but could not assimilate. In the letters they sent him was the implicit but clear invitation not to return. The signs of their continuing existence seemed reduced to a minimum: a short text appearing in a literary supplement, the mention of an author unknown to the rough and ready idols of the new generation, a story shared like a knowing wink among their own kind – these were apparently enough to make them feel they had not become obsolete.

In the railway station's noisily echoing hall, on the other hand, there was the sense of a humanity alive through its contradictions, a humanity both elemental and unpredictable. The crumbling British architecture, abandoned like the Empire that had created it, now welcomed an endless stream of dark-skinned, wary-eyed people from the provinces drawn to the capital in search of a different kind of poverty, a more alluring disenchantment. And as in all the railway stations the man of letters had known on two continents, here, too, there were plenty of aimless, hungry-looking young men available.

Only a few of them actually stole, or practised more or less gentle extortion. Most of them accepted the variously suggested "gift", the invitation to a bar beyond their usual expectations. Although they would never admit it, what they most appreciated were the conversations they had with these strangers, whose worlds they caught a fleeting glimpse of. They discovered scraps of experience to which they would never have any true access; the less naïve among them realised that it was only their youth and the explicit promise of virility that permitted them this fleeting insight into another life.

Among them, with them, the man of letters had discovered (apart from the occasional erotic service, which his meagre income would not often allow) a familiarity that was richer and more capable of surprise than friendships with his nostalgic compatriots, all of them prisoner to a Europe more longed for than remembered, or the polite indifference of the few native intellectuals aware of his presence in their country. The former tended to comment on the latest novel by Alexander Lernet-Holenia, which he had invariably not read, while the latter asked him for news of the "gruppe 47", of which he was equally ignorant.

During his first stroll through the station hall on this stiflingly hot, humid December night, he had seen a few of his acquaintances. One of them was leaning over a long-since emptied cup of coffee at the counter of a "drop-in café"; another was apparently absorbed in a recent crime portrayed on the cover of *As'* or *Hechos en el mundo*. He smiled or gave them a quick nod of the head, as though anxious not to interrupt whatever business they were involved in. Above all though, it was the pair of immense portraits, which had replaced other less overweening ones, that caught his attention.

He reflected yet again on the obscure links between the masses and those who believe they are manipulating them, the impalpable flow of power between the two extremes. In Vienna in 1938 he had seen a multitude of people, apathetic only a few days earlier, turn into a single-minded hydra baying its approval at the arrival of a nondescript *führer*. Now, in this young country that was equally sentimental and cynical, but lacking the imperial past which served in his homeland to feed the irony of its intellectuals and the rancour of its lower orders, family relations seemed to him to provide the model for its political structures: fathers who could be either doting or despotic, as easy to corrupt as they were quick to punish; mothers who according to legend could give milk even after their deaths, or who in reality, unable to produce their own children, declared that any unfortunate illegitimate child who acclaimed them was their own.

His attention had wandered in these reflections when he was startled to feel a hand on his shoulder. He turned his head and recognised Carlitos, a brown-skinned lad from the north, with sculpted cheek-bones and sleepy eyes. On a summer's night almost a year earlier, he had sneaked him into his rented room; then as now he was wearing a conscript's uniform that only served to underline the charms of a late adolescence subjected to rigours for which he was temperamentally unsuited. On this occasion his tone of voice was very different.

"I'm sorry, professor, but you should leave here at once. The police are down below with orders to round up at least a hundred . . ."

The unpronounced word hung in the air with the ghostly eloquence of the unspoken: yet another demonstration of the boy's natural delicateness — a year earlier he had asked, in an accent that sounded so enchanting to a Viennese ear: "Was that all right for you?", before folding a few banknotes with the portrait of General San Mart́n on them into his pocket. Tonight, before slipping away into the crowd, the man of letters squeezed his hand with the silent, heartfelt gratitude of someone who has escaped from other police raids under other skies and who knows, although he has not yet heard of a recent Broadway hit, that he too has always depended on the kindness of strangers.

★ ★ ★

Carlitos had learnt all he knew from Boneco da Silva. They had met in the third infantry regiment on the day they were both called up for military service. While their heads were being rapidly and carelessly shaved, Boneco looked down nonchalantly at the golden curls falling round his feet. "They'll have grown back in a month," he told his shearing companion, adding, to Carlitos' astonishment and admiration: "And in two, I'll be out of here . . . I know people . . ."

Their friendship took shape in the first days of their shared captivity. During their Saturday leave, as they were strolling through a dusty park full of bare trees, Boneco had gestured with his chin towards a fat man sweating in the shadow of a statue to Garibaldi. "Twenty minutes with that guy, and

I'll have enough to eat for three days . . ." Carlitos had not understood what he meant, but when scarcely half an hour later he saw Boneco re-appear with a smile and the words: "Come on, I'll pay", his admiration knew no bounds.

Sitting with a pizza and a litre of beer, Boneco's tongue loosened. Carlitos learnt that a barely concealed world of incident existed in the cracks and beneath the surface of this capital he was only just beginning to explore. Boneco "knew everything": his quicksilver grey eyes, halo of Venetian blond curls, nose squashed by a penalty he had not managed to hold on to, had all led him to be invited to the Rio carnival at the age of sixteen. He returned six months later, his original protector long since forgotten, apart from the affectionate nickname he kept as his *nom de guerre*, but with enough money saved to be able to move on from the room on the roof of his aunt's house where she let him stay. Even more important was the experience he had gained, which his natural intelligence and sociability soon put to good use. A fashion designer who worked for Sono Film wanted to show off his find by taking him to a *fiestita*, from which he emerged on the arm of a secretary to the Under-secretary of Information. A stupid accident cut short this *cursus honorem* apparently destined to overcome all obstacles on the way to ever-greater glories: a badly treated bout of what in those days was known as venereal disease aroused the anger of one of the regime's functionaries, and within a matter of days all the telephone numbers he had stored in a little blue notebook led him to communicate only with vague secretaries of people who were busy, away on business, or did not recognise his name. And the promised and desperately longed-for invitation to an intimate evening in honour of the North American sportsman Archie Moore never materialised.

Never for a moment did Carlitos doubt that this tawdry phoenix would rise from his ashes. He was convinced of this by the assurance with which Boneco spoke of high society and its celebrities, the ease with which he always declared himself to be above any fiction invented to impress him. Besides, he was a generous teacher: he advised Carlitos not to sell himself cheaply by frequenting railway stations or a certain café on a city-centre corner that got very busy after midnight, but was known in the trade as "Leftovers and Remnants". Carlitos did not always feel he could live up to this advice. His dark skin, cheap clothes, and provincial shyness made it impossible for him to go into the Frisco Bar so highly recommended by his friend. Whereas Boneco dreamt of a splendid comeback in Rio, without admitting it Carlitos would hang around the very places his companion had warned him against. Here he met people who it was true would be of no help in advancing him socially, and who did not offer him handsome rewards for his services, but made this orphan feel at ease: he listened to them, and could see they were glad for the attention he paid them.

It was Boneco who warned him one day that the police (he had been told by "someone in the know") had received orders to stage spectacular raids in order to instil in a credulous public the idea that the moral health of the nation was in danger. The President (unaware of the fact that only a few short months later he was to become the "deposed despot" for those same newspapers he at that moment controlled) in a delirium of omnipotence or (the versions differ) in a fit of premature senility, had decided to do battle against the Catholic Church, which ten years before had helped him in his irresistible rise.

A feature of that campaign was the re-opening of brothels that had for many years been illegal. The excuse: to contribute to the sexual education of the country's youth, by saving it from a pernicious chastity. A newsreel that was obligatory viewing in all the country's cinemas, included a "crime report" in which an exuberant rumba dancer yet to be operated on was denounced as the lover and presumed accomplice of an epileptic pickpocket. The yellow press was full of illustrations of freaks who were labelled as the corruptors of "our children".

That December night, protected by his uniform, Carlitos saw policemen beating, spitting on and then arresting several men who spent a few hours each day in the underground toilets at the railway station. He told himself that Boneco's friendship with the inspector at the 19th precinct was not simple boasting. As he returned upstairs, he recognised the professor – that was how he knew him and what he called him – the gentleman who spoke with such a funny accent and used such recherché words.

One evening the previous summer, when he could not come up with the money to pay him, the professor had asked him to dinner at a restaurant near the station, in a street that went up a hill round a well-known square. To Carlitos it seemed like somewhere he had only ever seen in the cinema: walls with dark wood-panelling, deer antlers hung symmetrically like hunting trophies, paintings with land-scapes of lakes and mountains. Other foreigners who were friends of the professor's came over to say hello, and he intro-duced Carlitos to them with great respect, and no hint of sarcasm or embarrassment. All the other gentlemen shook his hand and smiled warmly. With the help of a white wine that the professor called Moselle, it was not long before Carlitos felt himself part of a world where he had no need to feel ashamed of his rough manners or lack of conversa-tion. At the end of the evening, the restaurant owner refused to accept money, whispering something to the effect that "the professor's friends are our friends", and giving him a manly pat on the shoulder that lingered long enough to become sensual. "Come back whenever you like, young man. You'll be our guest."

Perhaps it was the memory of that evening, called to mind by the sight of the professor standing so lonely and at a loss in the station hall, that led Carlitos to warn him of the danger lurking underground.

"Professor, I'm sorry, but you must leave immediately. The police are below and they have orders to round up at least a hundred . . ."

He hesitated. None of the words he knew seemed appro-priate for the ears of such a well-educated man. He let the suspension marks say what he could not express as he might have wished, and let the hand on the professor's shoulder transmit all his sympathy.

* * *

This story has no plot, other than that of History itself. It is barely more than the impression left by an instant, a spark produced by two very different surfaces rubbing together. Perhaps the later destinies of those involved can serve in the way of narrative development.

Nothing more is known of Boneco da Silva after the end of his national service, which did not come about as quickly as he had prophesied, when he emigrated back to Rio de Janeiro, the scene of his early triumphs. But his role in the story was nothing more than as a useful prop. The instant this tale is trying to recall had only two protagonists.

Carlitos, once again following words of advice from Boneco ("Take it from me, in uniform you'll be a hit, without it, you'll be nothing"), had neglected to hand back his uniform the day he left the army and continued to wear it during his night-time escapades, until an occasion when a policeman stopped him and ordered him to identify himself. Convicted of "illegal wearing of a military uniform" and "falsely assuming a military rank", he was sent off to a jail in his own province, far from the bright lights of the capital.

His good conduct opened the possibility of a career in the police force. Appreciated for his dedication to the job, but considered rather soft, he was exempted from the use of the electric prod and from taking part in third-degree interrogations. That did not prevent him from attaining, with fewer teeth in his smile, and having lost the lustre of youth that had made him so popular during his brief career in the civilian world, the rank of police sergeant at the rather advanced age of forty-one. Over the years his fragile memory had led him to forget his friendship with Boneco, the worldy lessons he had given him, and above all the many gentlemen he had got to know thanks to those lessons. At the end of 1975 he was cut down by a burst of machine-gun fire during an attack by an armed band on the police station in which he served.

The man of letters never learnt of his demise. He had passed seventy years of age when a group of young Austrian writers, impatient with the little incestuous literary world of which they were a part, and perhaps curious to rediscover a minor figure of the past who was still alive, encouraged the Viennese city authorities to provide him with an apartment in a building where ageing, impecunious artists were housed. In this way, he received a one-way ticket and left the city where he had spent twenty-six obscure, poverty-stricken years, only to discover that the metropolis of the empire he had been born in was by now no more than the capital of a small republic.

In his new, extremely modest suburban home his neighbours were a retired dancer from the Kurt Joos company, whom he took care to avoid in the lift in order not to hear him protesting yet again about the changes made to the original choreography of *The Green Table,* and a dypsomaniac artist who devoted her declining years to creating hirsute tapestries of imprecise ethnic origin.

He often evoked the years spent on the far side of the Atlantic, and in these reveries Carlitos' name often surfaced, even if his features had begun to be confused with those of other to him equally exotic young men. In the dim and dull Vienna where he was soon to die, these memories of a nostalgic sensuality became almost unconsciously deposited in a volume of stories which for the first (and almost posthumous) time led to the award of a literary prize: in 1981 *Kleine Schwarze Köpfe* won the Café Havelka Preis.

From the window of the chauffeur-driven limousine sent to take him to the prize-giving ceremony, he saw neighbourhoods of Vienna he had not revisited since before his exile. He discovered, close by the gilded leaves of the dome of the Secession building, a Turkish immigrant market sprawling at the foot of façades decorated with glazed tiles by Otto Wagner. The astonishment he felt at this unexpected sight soon gave way to a feeling of pleasure. In all the excitement and nervousness he felt ahead of the ceremony, he remembered having heard on the radio that the incomprehensible world in which he found himself growing old had shortened distances and promoted migrations.

Out of commonplaces of this kind, he built comforting fantasies that stayed with him all the way to his moment of belated glory. Who could tell whether Carlitos might not be present among the audience awaiting him . . . Perhaps he would come up and thank him for dedicating this book he could not read to him. The professor shut his eyes and saw once again the printed words: "*Für Carlitos, Columbus meiner Amerika*".

OBSCURE LOVES

Place Saint-Sulpice

THE LOFTY BELLS OF SAINT-SULPICE CHURCH HAD ALREADY struck midnight, and the rectangle of the window – a mezzanine in the Rue Servandoni – was still lit. The man leaning against the bookshop window had been staring at this bare stage for more than two hours. He had seen two tall, slender, agile, young silhouettes come and go: no more than two black cut-outs, Chinese shadows that the light from the room inside projected onto the beige curtain; each time they came closer to it, their outlines became sharper, the black more intense. Whenever they moved back to the centre of the room, the silhouettes grew and became more diffuse, the black turned to fuzzy grey. These movements and occasional glimpses told him nothing about what was going on in the minuscule studio he had sometimes visited, with its electric cooking plate in an alcove, bathroom by the entrance, and a double mattress on the floor. At some moment the light would go off and he would need to see the two figures drop below the window to be sure they had gone to bed. Perhaps he was hoping to see some intimate gesture that would erase from his imagination the caresses and kisses which pursued him whenever he closed his eyes. "Reality can be horrible," he had thought more than once, "but it never hurts as much as what we imagine."

He remained motionless at his observation post, without feeling the cold, or looking at the increasingly rare passers-by who hastened past him on this January night. A strange quiet, an expectant silence seemed to suggest that it might start snowing at any moment. It was only when a voice inter-rupted this sense of expectation that his eyes left the window.

"Ralph! Where have you got to?"

It took him a moment to make out the man who had spoken these words and seemed to be drawing nearer. When his silhouette passed under a street-lamp, he could see the too-youthful gleam of his wig, how incongruous it looked above the dried-out, wrinkled skin.

"Did you see my Ralph?"

The man had come to a halt a few steps from him. He could see the wig was a deep walnut colour; under the lights, it shone as much as the clear varnish of his nails. The stranger did not give him time to consider his reply.

"My Ralph is a silver-grey cockerspaniel. He must be about four years old. I don't know what's wrong, but every time I take him out at night recently he escapes and hides. As if he were making fun of me. Then just as I'm about to start crying, he re-appears, or he waits for me, wagging his tail, in our doorway."

It was obvious that Ralph's owner's eyes were red-rimmed.

The watcher muttered an excuse: he had not been paying attention, and had not seen the dog go by. The stranger looked all round the square: no movement or noise betrayed the fugitive's hiding-place.

"Every night I say it's the last. I can't go on. You don't know all I've done for him. When I found him he was a stray scrounging left-overs in the Saint-Germain market. I bought him the best food. Thanks to me he grew into a strong, healthy dog. Later on, I gave him the meat I ate, first-class cuts, and God knows on my pension I can't afford many luxuries. And believe it or not, as soon as he gets out into the street, he starts sniffing at the first turd he comes across . . . And now this . . ."

He searched for some words of comfort, but they sounded clumsy, unconvincing, and his eyes registered a fresh movement by one of the two figures in the illuminated rectangle, although he could not be certain which of them it was.

"Don't try to console me, it's not worth it. If I had any sense, I'd have put him out in the street a long time ago. He deserves it. But I'm a poor fool, I'm too soft. Over-sentimental. Guess what I did for his last birthday? I took two of my mother's necklaces – oh, they were nothing special, one was jet, the other rock crystal – and had them sewn on his leather collar. Do you think he thanked me for it? The next Sunday at eleven o'clock mass, he was striding around showing off to all the bitches in the neighbourhood, without so much as a look at me . . ."

Still speaking, the stranger started to cry silently, though the tears did not affect his voice. As if he felt a sudden chill, he pulled up the collar of his coat, one of those popular garments known after the Second World War in France as a "Montgomery", in England as a "duffle coat". It was so threadbare it could well have been an original.

"You might say that once you reach a certain age, it's best just to accept things as they are. I know that, but I can't. I understand it with my head, but my heart keeps asking for a little affection. What am I supposed to do? Spend my evenings watching TV?"

This time the stranger stifled a loud sob. The watcher stretched out his hand and laid it on the shoulder of this person whose creased face suddenly seemed to contain the whole world's unhappiness. But he could not find any words to say. The other man smiled briefly, and gestured with his hand as if to suggest "don't bother", or "it's not worth it".

He watched him walk away without saying anything more. A few moments later he heard, from the shadows, the distant call of "Ralph!"

When he raised his eyes to the window again, it was dark. He had missed the precise moment when they had switched the light off, just as he had perhaps missed the probable, the dreaded shadow of the two entwined bodies slipping down towards the mattress which, he knew, was placed under the window.

For a few moments, he did not move. The fact that the bookshop whose window he leant against during his nightly vigils was called "La Joie de connaître" had long since ceased to amuse him. He thought, although he was not sure it was any comfort, that one of those two shadows might at that very moment be remembering how that same morning he had found a package in his letterbox, and inside the package a card with the words "Happy Birthday" printed on it in garish colours, and inside the card a folded handkerchief, and on this handkerchief the semen he had spilled onto the piece of cloth because he could not leave it where he would have wished.

Married Bliss

First of all she smothered her face and neck with a white substance that was milky rather than greasy, more liquid than solid. She spread it evenly with circular movements; then carefully removed it with a tissue that she dabbed everywhere once and sometimes twice if she noticed that any smudge of make-up still remained. Once she was satisfied that her face was clean, she used a cotton ball to smooth in a nourishing, revitalising cream. The result was an even shine which emphasised her weary look by giving it a feverish glow.

Her husband's flat, expressionless voice reached her from the bedroom.

"I'm very tired."

"Switch the light off. I won't be long. What time is it? I'm tired too."

"It must be three o'clock . . ."

"The others are going to stay up all night. Estela told me they're serving breakfast at seven."

"How much do you think the kids spent?"

"Less than we spent when they got married, that's for sure. Besides, there are three of them to pay for it. And we only have a golden wedding anniversary once in our life."

A grunt of agreement from the bedroom.

"What do you make of the Muñozes? I never thought they'd have the nerve to show up . . ."

"It was your idea to invite them . . ."

"Only so they wouldn't think we held it against them. But I never dreamt that they would show up. What a cheek!"

This time all she heard was a prolonged sigh.

"And what about Lidia's son? Who would have thought it, turning up with a girlfriend . . . it seems Doctor Allende was right when he said it was only a phase . . . his mother must be so relieved . . ."

The sigh was deeper, almost a groan.

"You can stop complaining, I've finished."

She switched off the bathroom light and went into the bedroom. Flat on his back on his half of the bed, her husband was already asleep.

As she came closer, she saw his eyes were open, and with something akin to a questioning look in them. She called to him several times, then felt his chest and leaned over his mouth. There was no sign of breathing. She stood motionless for a while, not knowing what to do; then, almost automatically, she moved towards the telephone and picked it up, only to replace the receiver almost at once. Her mind was full of threatening images: official notifications, having to look for papers that are never where you thought they were, children, daughters-in-laws and grandchildren invading the house; worse still, relatives, friends, a wake, the interminable vigil and having to say a few words to everyone, always feeling exhausted, never getting any sleep, having to dress up, go to mass, the funeral, all before she could be on her own, in silence, in bed . . .

She looked at the time. Almost four. She set the alarm for half past nine. She would tell them he died in his sleep, without her noticing.

She got into bed next to the lifeless body, lifted one of his arms and put it under her head. She lay down against his chest which – it was obvious now – was no longer rising and falling. She switched off the light and closed her eyes. Yes, a few hours sleep would help her face the coming nightmare: another family reunion, like the one she had had to put up with that night, but with no music, no laughter, only hushed voices and serious, if not sad, expressions on the same faces.

She wriggled closer to her husband, to feel protected by an embrace which, after all, was not that different from the one she had clung to every night for so many years.

The Second Time

Absorbed or absent, snared between impatience and tiredness, the expressions on the faces of the passengers in the *métro* had never ceased to intrigue him. (He still thought in terms of "*métro*" rather than "underground" even though it was fifteen years since he had come back from Madrid.) Whether they were studying the tips of their shoes or the destination map above the doors, scanning a book or letting their gaze wander through space without settling anywhere in particular, he always saw these faces as an interval, an involuntary interval in the staging of their lives to which these passengers were condemned. Between the departure and the arrival of their underground journey, in a dusty, indifferent light, they were free for a few moments from their bosses and clients, their spouses and children. Even their clothing, their hair or their make-up, all the marks of social identity, seemed suspended, waiting for the call to return them to the discipline of the stage.

In this limbo, he felt like an observer who could look on untouched, as if faced with patients still under the effects of anaesthesia, or a stealthy intruder into a mortuary . . . the punishment for this moment of vanity was not long in coming: he discovered in a pair of dark, over-made-up eyes, in a faintly ironic smile, that his gaze was being returned by someone else's, and that person's gaze brought him back to the nondescript tunnel between two stations on the Constitución to Retiro line from which only a moment before he had felt so aloof.

The woman was of indeterminate age or, as a kinder phrase has it, she was ageless. The heavy make-up was limited to her eyes and the brilliant scarlet of her lipstick; the pallid face and hair carelessly dyed an unconvincing black gave no suggestion of coquettishness. But there was about her a strangely theatrical emphasis, as if aimed at some distant spectator. She continued to stare at him, and he suddenly felt her gaze was just as ironic as her brief smile. Did she perhaps know him, and was she waiting for him to recognise her?

★ ★ ★

She had followed him since the morning without finding what seemed to her the right opportunity to make her presence known.

At nine he had left his apartment in Olivos and taken the train to Retiro; in the city centre he had gone into a bank and a government office to see to business; he had lunched on a sandwich and a glass of beer in a café on Calle Reconquista before going to Constitución to catch a train to Lomas de Zamora. He had spent almost two hours there, talking and negotiating in an estate agent's, before taking the train back to Constitución.

All these comings and goings did not surprise her. She knew that gradually over the years he had come to accept a practical, routine existence, far removed from the dreams they had thought they shared once upon a time. From a distance, unseen by him, she had watched as he slowly lost the impetuous tone of voice, the enthusiastic glint in his eye, his beaming smile.

★ ★ ★

When he boarded the train she was already in the carriage. He first saw her out of the corner of his eye, then noticed the dyed-black hair, the too intense scarlet of her lipstick, the way she looked at him as if waiting for a recognition that was a long time coming. "She looks so like her," he thought, and then: "Who knows what she would be like now, twenty years older and with all that's happened in between . . ."

At San Juan a lot of people got on, and for a while the woman was hidden by all the anonymous expressions of weariness and impatience. When he could see her clearly once more, she seemed still to be staring at him with the same air of absent-minded concentration, devoid of curiosity or acknowledgement. Several people standing between them got off at Independencia, giving him the chance to get closer. A faint smile crossed her lips again. In that instant, against all reason, he knew it was her.

"Don't look so astonished. I'm not dead, you know . . ."

She laughed, with the same spontaneity he recalled from so many years earlier. Just as he had then, he felt obliged to explain.

"I'm not so vain. Just because I don't see someone for years doesn't mean I think they must have died . . . but I'm amazed that it really seems as if time has stood still for you: you have that same light shining in your eyes. I, on the other hand . . ."

"I would have recognised you anywhere. Even, for example, if I saw you in the Stockholm Underground I would have recognised you."

"Where have you been all these years? Don't tell me you've been in Buenos Aires . . ."

"Where haven't I been! I've been travelling. A lot."

They fell silent. The surprise of meeting each other again had led to this sudden spurt of questions, but now they found that the lack of shared experiences left them with little more to say. Absent-mindedly, he observed the tearful beggar

106

woman from San Juan province who got on as always at Avenida de Mayo: a card round her neck declared in laborious and misspelt letters that she was a refugee from Kosovo whose husband and three children had been massacred by the Serb terror. At Diagonal Norte women with armfuls of flowers got off and other beggars got on: the man with a stump for a right arm, the other one with the sliced-off tongue that he poked out with a triumphant grunt.

"Have you been in Buenos Aires long? Are you going to stay?" he asked, for something to say.

"I've always been here. You were the one who left."

He insisted, more irritated by the fact that she had contradicted herself than really wanting to know the answer.

"I can't think why I didn't hear, why we've never run into each other."

"Perhaps because you never thought of me . . ."

Now she was smiling openly at him. "It's incredible how self-centred women can be," he thought, as so often in his life. This idea and other recollections distracted him for a few moments. When they reached San Mart́n he realised she was talking, almost nostalgically.

"I always remember that marvellous story you once told me. The one about the boy who one afternoon picks up a small coin on the beach, plays with it for a while, then throws it onto the sand. A short time later, as the last of the daylight is fading, he sees a city rise from the sea. Its architecture seems fabulous to him: it reminds him of illustrations he has seen in fairy tales. He strolls through streets lined with shops; impatient traders besiege him at their doors, offering him

107

silks embroidered with silver and gold, jewels, heirlooms, all for a coin, however small. One of the shopowners explains that the city, the richest of its time, was punished because of its inhabitants' greed. It was condemned to sink to the bottom of the sea with all its treasures, and to surface once every hundred years to offer them all for a single coin. Only when someone buys them will they be able to rest in peace. The boy looks for the coin in his pocket, then remembers he threw it onto the sand, because he thought it was worthless. He has to watch as the fantastic city sinks back into the sea, and realises he will be dead by the time it re-appears."

"She's confusing me with someone else," he thought, and also: "If I haven't seen her in all these years it must be because she was shut up in an asylum." They were walking up the steps to the train station at Retiro when he found an excuse he thought might sound convincing.

"Call me, I'm in the phone book. I have to catch a train now. See you soon!"

He began to run through the crowd. Without slowing up, he turned and waved at her; she was still staring at him with that faint smile that would stay in his memory: a Polaroid of this new separation that accompanied him through the entire journey back to his apartment.

* * *

It is this image that comes back into his mind several hours later, just before midnight, and leads him to break off his belated perusal of a newspaper about to become the previous day's, filled with supposed news that will soon be from the day before yesterday. He leans out of his window and instead

108

of the tranquil street and its silent foliage he sees a pallid face, oddly black hair, a bright red mouth.

He goes out for a walk, anticipating that the warm spring night will calm his nerves. All of a sudden, he comes to a halt as he remembers or understands something: "I never told her that story, I never mentioned Nils Holgersson to her. I'm sure of that. She couldn't know how much it affected me as a child." Immediately afterwards he recalls having read, heaven knows where, that in Santiago del Estero or in the Chaco, there is a belief that on the day of the dead they come back to the Earth to seek out their loved ones and try to take them off to the other world.

The clock on the small suburban station platform shows 23.56, but everyone knows they almost never work, and when they do they are either slow, or fast, or jerkily uncertain. On the far side of the tracks, he sees the light of an open bar and promises himself a geneva, something that always helps at difficult moments. He does not hear the 23.58 train arrive, and the shock of impact takes all sense of pain with it.

The image of a woman's face, faithful, stubborn, perhaps lovelorn, persists for . . . perhaps a second? But not even the most advanced chronometers can measure something already beyond time.

Love is lovelier
The second time around . . .

(Kahn and Van Heusen, sung by Pearl Bailey)

EMIGRÉ HOTEL

I

AT DUSK ON THE 3RD OF OCTOBER 1940, THE GREEK-
registered steamship *Nea Hellas* set sail from the port of Lisbon,
bound for New York. As the daylight faded, the lights of the
dwindling city appeared all the brighter, and when the ship
passed Belém, where a huge exhibition in the Praça do Império
had been inaugurated only a few weeks beforehand, a final
dazzling display lit up the darkness, creating a fantastic spectacle for those watching it from on deck.

A year earlier, this would have been a picturesque or joyful
moment. By October 1940, the passengers on the *Nea Hellas*
felt only a sense of loss and foreboding. Some of them have
written of their feelings: "The ship moved off in the darkness, slowly gathered speed and left the Tagus behind.
Suddenly, as if in a fairy tale, the Exhibition shone out. Its
magical lights were the last we saw of a Europe plunged into
misfortune" (Alfred Döblin). "A remarkable colonial exhibition had been staged at the waterside (. . .) My final look
back at Lisbon revealed the port to me. This was the last I saw
as we left Europe behind. The port seemed to me incredibly
beautiful. A lost love could not have been more beautiful"

(Heinrich Mann). "At midnight we saw the last lights of Europe, red as blood, sinking into the sea" (Hertha Pauli).

The *Nea Hellas* was one of the few ships which dared to make this crossing. A fortnight earlier, the Dutch ship *City of Benares* had been torpedoed by a German submarine. Among those drowned, together with her husband, was Monika Mann, whose brother Golo and Uncle Heinrich were now on board the Greek vessel. The idea of a ship leaving for the United States carrying not just these writers, but also Franz Werfel, Leon Feuchtwanger and their wives, as well as Alfred Polgar and Frederike Zweig, among other passengers less well-known but equally anxious to avoid the Second World War, has an almost comical element to it.

Their forced seclusion on the ship, and the fact that they were neighbours whether they liked it or not, brought out petty vanities and rivalries, hushed at times of even relative peace. The fleeting and ambiguous coincidence that they were anti-fascist and had sufficient funds to pay the extravagant price of a berth on this modest vessel, had turned them into a repertory company on an impromptu tour, playing the role of the last scions, emissaries, or survivors of European culture in the unconsciously mocking spotlight of a name like *Nea Hellas* . . . a distant relative of the medieval ship of fools? *Ein neues narrenschiff*?

The last lights of Europe being extinguished in the night is one of those striking metaphors occasionally offered by experience: that night of the 3rd of October, at the height of Nazism's triumphs, Europe as the hearth, or the mother, abandoned in her hour of need for an unknown length of time, which none of them in their heart of hearts wanted to be for ever . . . Uncertainty, anxiety, relief, nostalgia, remorse: an extensive catalogue of emotions is at hand for anyone who wishes to evoke this moment of a collective adventure.

The painful irony lies in the fact that those "last lights" the emigrants saw slipping into the distance, signalling goodbye to a world that had been theirs and which they suddenly now saw converted into an irretrievable, inaccessible past, shone from the Exhibition of the Portuguese World, in which General Salazar's Estado Novo was celebrating 800 years of Portugal's existence as an independent nation. This sumptuous array of handicrafts and vegetation, of natives and cookery of Angola, Mozambique, Goa and Macao, had the slogan "If there had been more world, we would have reached it", inscribed on an art déco pediment no less authoritarian in style than Berlin's Olympic Stadium, Paris' Place du Trocadéro, or the monuments Stalinism bestowed on the capitals of its satellite republics. The ostentatious waste of electricity, emblem of Portugal's neutrality, was a celebration not only of a patriotic anniversary but also of the wisdom, even cunning, of a ruler whose subtle manoeuvres are more easily appreciable sixty years on than they were in 1940. In those days he was a fascist, and it was from fascism that all these people were fleeing, aghast at the enormity of the loss that this abandonment of Europe suddenly confirmed, but impressed despite themselves by the glittering display of a triumphal exhibition of imperial power.

I am sitting on the terrace of the Ninho das Aguiais *pension*.
Spread out in front of me is a map of Lisbon which I thought
I would need for my first visit here. From it I can see that
this terrace dominates the city: the hill of Nossa Senhora de
Graça is almost opposite, a bit to the right; further off I can
make out the lesser heights of the Eduardo VII park and São
Pedro de Alcántara; down below I can see the chequerboard
of the Marquis de Pombal's city, and the elegant geometry
of the Terreiro do Paço by the water's edge; behind me I know
there is the castle of São Jorge, with this little hotel halfway
up the hill towards it; down at my feet lies what the guidebook calls the "Moorish maze" of Alfama.

The fact is I did not need the map. I even know where the
places I cannot see from the terrace are situated: up beyond
the Bairro Alto is Lapa, and further off still, the road out to
Belém. During the month of daily visits I made to the Leo
Baeck Institute in New York, I learned to place all these names
on the imaginary model I constructed in my mind thanks to
other maps, some of them ancient, and especially the count-
less tales told of the city by others. I can for instance pinpoint
the Via Aurea in the Baixa where one afternoon in 1940 my
grandfather ran into Annette Kolb. She was looking for a
jeweller to sell her rings and buy a ticket being sold at three
times the normal price for a seat on a plane (in those days
called a "clipper") for New York. And I know the German
bookshop in Rua Duque de Palmela that was the unwitting
witness to Heinrich Mann's irritation when he found not one

of his own titles on shelves packed with his brother's books.

It was this grandfather of mine whose papers I had gone to study at the Leo Baeck Institute. Five heavy cardboard boxes were stuffed with his notebooks, letters and many original manuscripts, most of them fragments, carbon copies on almost evanescent "onionskin" sheets of paper. There are also envelopes marked "miscellanea" which contain business cards, photos of people I cannot identify, tickets and train timetables which do not mean much to me either (the most frequent being: Lisbon-Estoril-Cascais) as well as a programme from the Politeama cinema for the 17th of May 1945, when *Casablanca* was first screened in Portugal.

My grandfather was not a well-known author, and I doubt whether there will be any posthumous re-evaluation of his worth. His papers are not consulted as are those of say, Joseph Roth, and if the Institute agreed to store those five boxes, it must be because my grandfather knew many less-forgotten writers. With them he took part in the flight from the Third Reich to refuges that soon proved insecure; in 1940, like many others, he finally arrived in Lisbon, from where he hoped to be able to take a boat — riskier than a plane, but less expensive — to America.

Sixty years later, in the silent, welcoming gloom of the Institute broken only by the clear pools of light over each table seat, I examined these still intact papers, written in ink that has not yet faded. Evening after evening, when I emerged into the noise, the disgruntled passers-by and the soaring buildings of 73rd Street, I did not feel as if I were returning to my own world, my own time. Above and beyond a family history that two years previously I had no interest in, and only a few months ago realised might be the means of obtaining a grant, Lisbon and 1940 had almost immediately taken hold of me. Thanks to that family history and that grant I arrived in the city yesterday. I intend to stay a month.

Before breakfast this early spring morning, I discovered this terrace, and decided it will be where I work each day from now on. In my room I left all the notebooks and files where I had more or less arranged the hundreds of photocopies I had made. My computer is stored in New York; in my pocket I carry a notebook and two ball-point pens, which seem to me more appropriate to the work I am doing. On this first morning of my stay, I woke up very early, unable to contain my enthusiasm, my desire to uncover the mysteries and treasures that for me, and only me, are buried in this city I watch slowly awaken as the golden mists lift over the waters of the Tagus.

3

My grandmother was called Anne Hayden Rice. To the dismay of her family, people of old money and with gardens stretching down to the Hudson in the north of New York State, at the age of twenty-eight and after showing a marked disinclination to get married, she had enrolled in the Lincoln Brigade, one of the many international divisions fighting on the side of the Republic in the Spanish Civil War. In Valencia and Barcelona she was witness to the intrigues of the Stalinists trying to expel socialists and anarchists from the Republican Front, not baulking at denunciations and summary executions to achieve their goal. Her puritan conscience was beginning to be revolted by the tactics of *realpolitik* when she met a pair of German volunteers she was to share her life with from that moment on: Theo Felder and Franz Mühle. A few years younger than her, they had been art students in Berlin before National Socialism rose to power, forcing Theo's family to seek refuge in Basel. Franz was not Jewish, and so could stay on in the "Athens on the Spree" in spite of his disgust at the proliferation of swastikas, jackboots on city pavements, or posters in the entrance to cinemas and cafés declaring them to be *juden-verboten,* all of which reminded him, in simultaneous bursts of shame and relief, of his distant yet present friend, who wrote to him assiduously from the Swiss side of the Rhine. The powerful if ill-defined enthusiasm aroused by the Spanish Civil War, based more on anti-fascist sentiment than on any precise ideas, gave them the chance to meet again in an adventure worthy of their dreams. Ineffectual, lacking in discipline, they met up in Barcelona, and it was there that they came to know Anne, perhaps the only woman capable of bridging (what I suspect may have been) their tacit desires. Was it perhaps (what I suspect may have been) her tacit desires which led her to be the bridge between two men she could not have loved individually? After the defeat of the loyalists, Anne had no problem travelling, and was able to return to the family residence in Albany; if before it had seemed narrow to her, now it seemed as airless as a sanatorium. Theo and Franz crossed the Pyrenees, only to be swiftly interned by the French authorities. For the French army, the Second World War did not last long; to the two friends, the defeat and occupation of France simply meant a change of label: whereas before they had been undesirable aliens, then enemy aliens, now they were German Bolsheviks, destined for a less porous prison camp than those the French organised. Early in the summer of 1940 they paid some guards to look the other way for a few moments; they crossed back over the Pyrenees on foot, only weeks before this same crossing became a profitable business for anyone who knew the trails and mountain passes well enough to call himself a *passeur*; under protective night skies they travelled on back roads across Catalonia, Valencia and Andalusia, until one dawn found them in Ayamonte, from where they crossed the Guadiana on a barge to Vila Real de Santo António. The pilot, pleased to be called captain repeatedly by these two exhausted foreigners who nevertheless made the effort to speak Spanish, hid them from the prying eyes of the Civil Guard on the back of a vehicle where they spent the interminable twenty minutes of the river crossing curled up in each other's arms. After several minutes of clicks, screeching, indistinct murmurs and distant thunderclaps, they heard Anne's voice: she arranged to meet them in Lisbon, and promised them that money would arrive "as soon as possible" at the United States consulate.

All this I know. These are facts documented in my grandfather's letters and notebooks, in stories my mother heard and passed on to me years later. The only things I have invented are their emotional ties — possibly banal ones, like everything we use to explain human behaviour – but which serve to help me conjure up these beings from a past I know only through literature. There remains one element of mystery. One day in 1940, Anne and Theo were married in the United States consulate in Lisbon, and left immediately for New York. Franz stayed on in Portugal.

For me, this raises endless questions – each question immediately prompting another one. Did my grandmother choose which of them to marry? Was it her friends who decided? Was it a marriage of convenience? Or perhaps of love? What happened to Franz? The welcoming but mute boxes in the Leo Baeck Institute contain only two letters he sent from Portugal during the Second World War, and nothing thereafter. What could have become of him, possessing either no papers or invalid ones, in a country he had not chosen and whose shaky neutrality he might have reason to fear would not last forever? How did the friends experience their separation? How had they taken the decision? What had gone wrong between them? They had written each other enthusiastic letters every other day when they were in Basel and Berlin; in order to meet up again they had made use of a foreign war, in which they fought hoping to destroy the very idea of nationality; they had shared heaven knows what intimacy and complicity with the intrepid and challenging North American woman who was to become my grandmother . . .

There had been a falling out, I am sure of it.

4

Albany, 3rd of September 1940

My dear ones:

There's really no reason for you two to stay on at the uncomfortable *pension* you describe in your letter. The fact that at the back of your wardrobe you found a torn and threadbare leather jacket with a Hungarian passport missing its photograph in the pocket could make an excellent opening for a novel, if one day Franz gets tired of playing at politics and decides to devote himself properly to something he is much better at . . . But this discovery, which I guess will not be repeated, is no reason for you to stay on between walls saturated with the smell of grilled sardines, if not the even more persistent stench of cod.

The vice-consul taking this letter to Lisbon for me has also got a letter of credit which will allow both of you to live and eat without fuss at the Palace Hotel in Estoril. I'm assured it is the best there is, and if it doesn't seem too frivolous to you, you might even venture to the nearby beach. Take care when swimming, boys!

After the good news, the less good – though it is not as bad as we might have feared. At the moment, United States immigration visas are hard to come by, even by pulling all the strings that my father – who exceptionally in this case is one hundred per cent behind me — is able to pull. Even a marriage at this time between a couple like us (by which I mean between myself and one of you: the US authorities would not permit any fancy arithmetic) is regarded with suspicion, and they would demand of the foreign husband (especially if he has lost his original nationality) a lengthy waiting period before they authorised his entry into this paradise of ours . . . On the other hand, a lot of institutions are mobilising to save Jews in danger . . .

Franz: I know it won't be easy to accept this, but in circumstances such as these, Theo has an advantage. (Who would ever have thought that being a Jew could have its privileges!) We can talk it over in more detail as soon as I arrive. For the time being I just want you to know what the situation is here, and to understand what possibilities there are for immigration.

I'll never forget that night in Valencia, the power cut, the air-raid sirens, that half bottle of rum we found in the sideboard of the abandoned socialist committee headquarters, and my promise never to try to separate you: it would always be the three of us, never two plus one. So, please think it over. If a decision has to be taken, you two take it without my getting involved.

In two or three weeks at most, I'll be there with you again. There are moments when this all seems like the final disaster — Europe, this war, everything we were fighting for . . . but anyway, if the world is about to end, let's spend a moment together before it does; if it is to go on spinning, it's up to you two to decide the future.

I love you guys

Anne

5

"Anything goes . . . just look at the clothes they're wearing, the way they behave . . . As for their bodies! Anything goes now . . . some days I miss the hotel, but the hotel as it used to be; don't for a minute think I'd still like to be working in what Estoril has become these days."

Don Antonio Carvalho waved vaguely with his right hand, perhaps to indicate the plebeian public stretched out on the sand of the beach resort, or the still impressive and recently renovated bulk of the Palace Hotel; or possibly he was simply wafting away the smoke from his Craven A cigarette, the second or third he had smoked since we had met half an hour earlier.

It was five in the afternoon, but on this first hot day of April that seemed like a foretaste of summer, a noisy, enthusiastic crowd had launched itself onto the beaches around Lisbon with the single aim of exposing as much of their bodies as the laws permitted to the sun's rays.

"In those days, a beach like the Tamariz was an elegant place, you were among the best sort of people. For example, those of us who worked in the hotels were not even allowed in . . . the ladies and gentlemen did not want to be seen with the staff. Friends of mine who still work at the Palace tell

122

me that now a Dutch family has their nanny sitting at table with them, and that she chooses her own food . . . Everything is like that . . . the casino is full of slot machines, and the only proper gambling saloon lets in women wearing trousers . . ."

It was hard to steer the conversation, or rather the monologue, in any particular direction. Like many old men, Don Antonio was sure he knew what interested the other person, and would not let himself be deflected if that other person dared express an interest in people or things he did not consider worthy of attention. I asked him if "in those days" the political leanings of the guests were common knowledge.

"What can I say . . . if a Viennese doctor couple by the name of Becker was here waiting for entry visas to the United States and rarely left their room, there wasn't much doubt about it. But all those who were desperate to reach the United States were gone by the start of '41, and those who were left, or came afterwards, were not so easy to pigeon-hole. I can remember one businessman, the representative of an import-export company, who would often go to Dublin for a few days, and to Berlin as well . . . another, a Romanian with an Argentine passport, slept all afternoon and only woke up when the Casino opened; then one fine day he vanished, leaving behind nothing but his gambling and hotel debts; some time later, the German embassy paid them all off. Are you North American?"

I did not bother to correct his impression. I had no desire to tell a stranger my family history, in which not even members of the same generation had been of the same nationality, and where all of them had held more than one passport. And besides, I had explained to him I was doing work for a North American foundation. Before I had time to lie, Don Antonio went on:

"In those days I knew a writer from your country. He spent months at the hotel: Prokosch was his name. I know that's German, but he was North American. He was a writer: he noted everything down. A lot of people said he was a spy, but I think a spy would have made some kind of effort to disguise what he was doing, don't you? Sometimes he even paid me, nothing extravagant, just good tips, to tell him about other guests. I reckon he was looking for material for his novels. He was a real gentleman, in fact: always impeccably dressed, and he spoke several languages. He could be ironic, too. He used to say: "You are the ones who are winning this war." He meant that everyone in Portugal took advantage of the presence of so many foreigners. The 1939 season, when war broke out, had been disastrous, but even before the autumn of 1940, when business was at its peak, people in Estoril were paying a fortune just for an armchair to sleep in. The Atlantic Hotel opened up rooms in its attic, and put beds in the bathrooms. Even the most humble *pensions* proudly hung 'No vacancies' signs on their doors . . ."

All at once Carvalho seemed tired. His voice became thick and he slurred over words that were not especially difficult. I observed the classic smartness of his clothes, the care he had taken to trim his moustache and the discreet way he had disguised its white hairs, something he did not have to bother with on the top of his head, which was already bald.

It was still scorching in the sun, and his skull shone. I offered him a glass of port, but he preferred a whisky (or a scotch, as he called it). I asked whether he would prefer to go to the English Bar or the one in the Palace Hotel; he chose to return to the scene of his memories. Before we went in, he dabbed lightly at his brow with a turquoise-coloured handkerchief.

The hotel bar seemed to me sufficiently nondescript to save it from any hint of pretention. But as he sipped his drink, Carvalho gazed around the room in an unimpressed way in which I sensed disapproval. I anticipated his reservations.

"It's not like it used to be in those days?"

"Just look: the velvet curtains are synthetic. All right, so this table is made of wood, but formica can't be far away."

6

I find it hard not to laugh when I read that in her eventful if never disastrous exile, the insufferable Alma Mahler (in Lisbon in 1940 she was Alma Werfel, previously Alma Gropius) dragged with her more than a dozen trunks stuffed with belongings she considered indispensable, most of which went astray on French trains between Bordeaux, Saint-Jean-de-Luz and Marseilles, as a result of a confusion between the dates of her visas and tickets. For her, Lisbon was a simple parenthesis. Whereas Döblin or Mann paid some affectionate attention to this city, even though they were too distraught to appreciate it for itself, or for any existence it might have beyond the fleeting presence of all these refugees, the only thing the fearsome conjugal muse remembered about it was the theft of some English pounds by a Viennese swindler and the timely aid offered by a hotel porter. Perhaps she deplored, as much as the ghastly food on board the *Nea Hellas*, the lack of an adequate stage on which to show off the personality of her latest husband. With her previous spouses, she had learnt that this was the only light she could aspire to, the only way she could create the illusion that her own hypothetical talents really existed.

7

There appears to be no mention in the Portuguese newspapers of the disappearance of Berthold Jacob on the 25th of September in Lisbon. I discovered this name, usually as no more than a passing reference, in the lists ("Emigration", "Exile" and many others) produced by researchers in the former German republics, in the days when the Federal Republic and the so-called Democratic Republic were competing to set the record straight on their common past.

Perhaps it is only justice that Jacob's disappearance should leave no trace at the time. As a journalist, he had devoted himself to publishing what the newspapers would not print, to proclaiming "the other side" of the news. Born in Berlin, he was nineteen in 1917 when, like so many other assimilated Jews in both the Prussian and Austro-Hungarian empires, he enlisted as a volunteer in the First World War. A year later, he returned a militant pacifist. He became friends with Kurt Tucholsky and Carl von Ossietky, literary figures who had taken up politics. In 1929 he was condemned to eight months in prison for "treason", after one of the many trials his articles laid him open to: his favourite target was the clandestine re-armament of Germany, financed by heavy industry, and in defiance of the Treaty of Versailles. In 1933, the arrival in power of the National Socialists forced him into exile. He chose to live in Strasbourg, the closest he could get to Germany in France, and from there continued to write and to publish bilingual magazines in which he tried to stir his readers' conscience against the regime that had triumphed in his country and aimed to do the same in the rest of Europe.

In 1935 he received an irresistible summons: two of his compatriots who had recently taken exile in Basel had some secret documents to give him about German re-armament. At the Swiss border station he was met by an emissary who said he had been sent to take him to the house where his fellow countrymen had sought refuge. Possibly Jacob was unaware that the suburbs of Basel, situated on a bend in the river Rhine between France and Germany, actually spilled over into both countries. The car he got into took many twists and turns, crossed several bridges over the river, and finally left the disorientated passenger on the German side of the invisible border, where Gestapo agents were waiting to bustle him off to Berlin.

For the one and only time in all those years, the Swiss government made a formal complaint about the violation of its territory, and for the one and only time in those years, the Third Reich yielded. On his return to France, the worse for wear but still undaunted, Jacob continued with the mission he had set himself until September 1939 when, at the outbreak of the new war everyone had feared so greatly, the French government interned him along with all other foreigners of "enemy" origin. Escapes, hiding places, false documents, the trek from Marseilles to Madrid and then in August 1941 arrival at Lisbon were chapters in his adventure, as they were for so many others.

The Gestapo could not allow its prey to escape, above all by legal means. A month later, Gestapo agents kidnapped Jacob a second time, and took him to Berlin via Madrid, where the German Lufthansa provided all the air services. A cell in the Alexanderplatz, a show trial, his hospitalisation "for health reasons": Jacob's story becomes lost in secondary sources. The last mention of him is on a list of patients in the Berlin Jewish hospital, which records his death in February 1944.

Why does this person intrigue me so? I have never dedicated myself to either political militancy or "campaigning" journalism; in fact even when I share their opinion, I am often irritated by the air of moral superiority assumed by those who pursue these careers like a vocation. Can it be because there are so many small details which link this sad story with the almost frivolous one of my own grandparents? Theo Felder and his family were staying in the opulent, aristocratic city of Basel, with its hidden mysteries and porous frontiers, at the time when Jacob was kidnapped. Franz Mühle had known Tucholsky as a student, and had even sung songs written by the poet . . . During the short month that Jacob could breathe freely in Lisbon, had the two ever run across each other?

Beyond all this idle speculation, I can sense once again my predilection for obscure characters. "Just as in the cinema, in real life there are stars and supporting actors." "Every life is made up of intersections with other lives." These quotations help suggest why I prefer my grandparents and someone like Jacob to all the more famous people who were in Lisbon at the same time.

8

Some nights I am overcome by a strange sensation that I can only define as cultural nausea.

I am surprised to find myself wishing I knew nothing about this city, especially about the people who passed through it in those days of 1940 that seemed to offer no tomorrow. The name of a street, or even of a café or hotel, immediately conjures up the writer, a historical character or an episode from a novel, which are always there at the back of my mind.

This Lisbon I am visiting for the first time in the spring of the year 2000 seems to me a comparatively prosperous city, pleased to be part of the European community. Beyond that, in its indolence, I can sense an atavistic city that escapes the commonplaces of its modern-day appearance: an ancient capital, proud and humiliated, hidden in the folds of a topography of cybercafés, easily accessible drugs, and "techno-music" on all sides. I glimpse it like those sudden crevices that emerge between two buildings, long, deep gashes that sometimes reveal the distant river, and more often are stamped with the tracks of vehicles called *ascensores*, somewhere between a tram and a cablecar.

In the same way as every city that at the end of the twentieth century has decided to cash in on its image, Lisbon has transformed its past glories into tourist attractions. The visitor who has his photograph taken next to the bronze statue of Pessoa as they both sit at a table outside the Brasileira café in Chiado, has quite possibly never read any of his poems; and even if the literary supplement of his newspaper has told him something about the heteronyms, it is probable he has no idea how far the extraordinary uniqueness of Pessoa's work is typical, in its singularity, of the fate of the nation which gave birth to the author, and of the city where he vegetated in such an obscure fashion. To me, Lisbon is a palimpsest in which my grandfather's journey connects with those of a host of other people, only a few of whom he ever knew . . . I think of all those refugees from Central Europe or Germany, or from the Slav countries, waiting impatiently in their consulates or besieging the travel agency counters. What did they know about Portugal? What did Lisbon mean to them? It was no more than a starting point — picturesque perhaps, certainly never intended — a city where food was not rationed and one could eat as in the good old days, enjoy the nightly display of electric lights that the capitals they had fled from could no longer allow themselves . . . Did they ever meet any Portuguese during their stay?

But these people are the subject of my research. Many a night when I leave the Antigo Restaurante 1º de Maio: Cozinha Caseira, in Rua de Atalaia, I would love to banish them from my mind and be able to surrender myself unthinkingly to the gentle evening breeze, which among other things brings with it the smell of fresh sardines grilling a golden brown on a charcoal burner, or something as delightful to me as the perfume of jasmine or honeysuckle. Yet it is an illusion to think that I can give myself up to pure sensations, that they can take me out of myself. My Lisbon is a ghost city, and it is enough for me to spot a faded sign (Pensão Velha Praga?) to drag me back to my dialogue with the shades.

9

Lisbon, 15th of October 1941

Dear friends,

It's been more than a year since our separation, and I often wonder whether Anne's lovingly sacrilegious idea has borne the expected fruit. Nine months should have been enough to find out if a double paternity is possible, or if the child's features betray the presence of one factotum or the other . . . but that would mean entering into a correspondence, and I have no wish, for the moment at least, to reveal my name and address to the postal censorship services. I think that a name and a document are not all that can be given out of love. Rather than succumb to the kind of sentimentality bound to irritate Anne's Anglo-Saxon sensibility – capable though of such unorthodox initiatives as the one I mentioned – I prefer to remain ignorant of the outcome, if there was one, of the pact we made in room 215. Why then am I writing to you? Possibly simply to tell you I am alive. Despite all the difficulties and uncertainties, I feel fine here. I hope this will not shock you, but I always put my trust more in culture than in politics. Allow me to quote Professor Wennerström, whom we met in the hotel and who knew what he was talking about: "Better Portugal with fascism than Sweden with democracy".

See you soon, perhaps.

L'Anonimo Berlinese

10

In the Cascais municipal archives there are some fifteen thousand records on foreigners kept by hotels in Estoril and Cascais. From them I learn that Franz Mühle and Theo Felder shared room 213 in the Palace Hotel from the 10th of September to the 2nd of October 1940; Anne Hayden Rice rented room 215 from the 26th of September to the same 2nd of October. She is recorded as being North American, Franz as German and Theo as *statenlos* (stateless?).

On the 3rd of October the *Nea Hellas* left Lisbon bound for New York . . .

The director of the archives, whom I had imagined to be unapproachable, speaks fluent English and Spanish. She listens to me so politely it seems she has nothing else to do. In her office, with the blinds filtering the almost summer-like sun on this April afternoon, I could spend hours listening to her stories in the cool half-light. Despite her youth, she refers to those distant days with quiet authority, as if she had lived them herself.

"Just as not all the Germans registered were supporters of the Reich (remember it was only Jews who were stripped of their nationality by decree), it is understandable that in the climate of neutrality imposed by the Portuguese authorities – and which the management of the different hotels was keen to uphold – meetings took place between people that would have been unimaginable elsewhere."

"Could it be said that each hotel had its political sympathies or antipathies?"

"Not exactly. At the Palace, although the owners were Portuguese, the manager was an Englishman: George Black. Perhaps that's why the hotel got the reputation of being pro-ally. That did not prevent – or even perhaps inspired as a challenge – the German ambassador Von Hüne organising a banquet there in honour of Rommel's victories in North Africa. And the fact is that the ambassador frequently dined at the Palace."

The archive director smiles faintly before adding:

"He preferred a sparkling Portuguese wine, our São Miguel, from Mealhada, to French champagne."

"What about the other hotels?"

"The Atlantic was supposed to be pro-German, possibly because in the thirties that was where German naval officers stayed when they were in port at Lisbon. In 1941, a man reputed to be Hitler's private secretary spent three days in the hotel; afterwards the rumour got out that his mission had been to meet emissaries from Roosevelt to negotiate a bilateral peace. And during those years Ribbentrop, Count Ciano and Admiral Canaris all stayed at the Atlantic . . ."

A hint of irony tinges her imperturbable objectivity.

"To even things up, I think we should say that Stefan

133

Zweig was also registered as staying at the hotel in 1938 . . ."

"Could you tell me whether, after the 2nd of October 1940, the names of Mühle or Felder are recorded in any other hotel besides the Palace?"

The records may be handwritten on crumpled cardboard, but their contents have already been entrusted to the intangible memory of a computer. The director searches on her screen, discreetly located on a low table next to her desk. After several manoeuvres and what seems to me like an interminable pause, she looks at me. The smile has gone from her face, and I realise that to her I am no less of a curiosity than the people in her archive are for me.

"On the 2nd of October 1940, Felder and Mühle left the Palace. That is the last record we have of those two names."

11

"At dawn on the 23rd March 1941 timid rays of sunlight were piercing the mists over the Tagus when the Lisbon police pulled the body of an unidentified man from the monotonous, lethargic waters lapping at the pier by the Terreiro do Paço. The man (around forty years old, tall, thin, with receding brown hair, almond-shaped eyes, prominent cheekbones) could be hard to identify: the only clue lay in a label sewn into his suit lining: J. Druskovic, *tailleur*, Zagreb. But his pockets contained a wealth of other identities: sixteen passports issued by the Argentine embassy in Berne, with plausible stamps and signatures, but one glaring omission: the photograph of the person whose identity the papers were supposed to confirm."

(This fragment, typed on a loose sheet of paper, does not

correspond to any article in the newspapers of the time, or any entry in my grandfather's notebooks. I think it could be the start of a novel never written, or perhaps lost. Could Theo have sent it, or taken it with him when he emigrated? And what if Franz Mühle was the man who entered the United States as Anne Hayden Rice's husband, with a passport in the name of Theo Felder?)

12

This afternoon I decided not to visit the Municipal Library, where I am sure my absence will not be felt by the enormous bound volumes of the 1942 newspapers. I have reached the siege of Stalingrad, and I already know the seven months it lasts will be fateful for the German troops. I can sense — although perhaps this is due to the light my reading throws onto unremarkable reports with the hindsight of more than half a century — that the wind is changing. Perhaps the vendors of *Signal*, a German illustrated weekly published in several languages to spread epic, optimistic images of a Europe rescued from parliamentary decadence, are no longer touting their magazine at the outside tables of the Pastelaria Suiça. Leaning on their piles of magazines proclaiming the glorious deeds helping build a New Europe, perhaps they now await their faithful clients a few metres away in the centre of the Plaza Rossio, among the crippled bootblacks and amateur beggars clustered at the foot of the statue to Pedro IV, who was to become Pedro I after being exported to Brazil as emperor . . .

Brazil . . . In February 1942, Stefan Zweig had committed

suicide during the Rio carnival. And yet it seems to me that only a few weeks later back in Europe people could start to breathe again. But I must correct myself at once: if such a hope did exist, it was false. The reversals of fortune at Stalingrad merely exacerbated the Third Reich's theatrical passion for creating a real life apocalypse. A sort of Oberammergau passion in reverse? (I wonder if it takes generations of rustic actors who put on their own sacred story to make this other kind of performance possible: vengeance and exorcism for the holy version, set not in an idyllic Tyrol but in a nightmare camp, and showing the eternal face of modern industry and work: the slavery of disposable lives.) Were Auschwitz, Maidanek and Treblinka the other side of some shining souvenir medallion from Oberammergau?

In 1940, in Lisbon and Estoril, the most refined French prose writer of his age had observed the chaos of exodus with a gaze still tainted by a worldly, aesthetic racism: "The Jews are the ones who talk the loudest, who call to each other in Portuguese, who shout in Portuguese: 'What lovely weather! What wonderful *vinho verde*', doubtless to create the impression that they feel at home, that a week in Lisbon has turned them into Lusitanian Jews, the Jewish nobility, the ones who did not vote for the death of Jesus. They hurry past the bus bringing Jews from Switzerland by a clandestine route that avoids (although it adds fifty leagues to the journey) the crossroads where young farmhands throw stones at its windows. These new arrivals stumble from their bus with downcast eyes, lifeless hair, still speaking French, English or German. They were the ones who did vote . . ."

In July 1942, in Paris, Heydrich ordered René Bousquet to organise the round-up in the Vél'd'hiver. In 1944, in Hungary, the weak fascist Admiral Horthy was about to be replaced by a puppet government; his son had been kidnapped and sent to Mauthausen as a means of blackmailing the ageing regent if he refused to authorise the entry of German troops into Hungarian territory in a last, futile stand against the Soviet advance. For good measure, the last-gasp regime in Hungary decided to deport the Jews to extermination camps. Prior to this, they had been crammed into ghettos and excluded from all the professions, but had not had to face the "final solution"; in January 1945 in Budapest, tired of the delays of German bureaucracy, the local militants of the cross made of arrows threw every Jewish person they could identify into the freezing waters of the Danube.

No, the retreat from Stalingrad represented nothing more than a military defeat. The final years of the inferno would be the cruellest of all for those condemned to suffer it.

This afternoon I have forsaken the gloom of the library for the blinding glitter of sunlight on the estuary waters. I am on the Santa Lucia esplanade, sitting at a table with a chessboard engraved on it. The old men who are regulars will be here soon, some of them shuffling along in slippers and pyjama bottoms, others in dark suits pressed as impeccably as their spotless white shirts; this difference in styles will not prevent them sharing a game that only nightfall can bring to an end. It is a warm May afternoon, and the perfume from the wistaria smothering the pergolas is borne on the breeze. In the distance, boats are plying between the two banks of the Tagus, or heading out into the Atlantic. This spring of the year 2000 becomes confused in my mind with that of 1942, whose yellowing traces I should be sifting through at this very moment in the library: the same strong light, doubtless the same chess players, the same profusion of wistaria.

Is it only a few proper nouns, a few geographical details, and above all, the identity of the victims, that has changed?

13

Lisbon, 25th of November 1942

Dear Anne, dear . . . Theo?

I hope these lines reach you before Christmas. I'll be celebrating it too, and not just to conform to my new identity. Even though we were not sufficiently assimilated to put up a fir tree and decorate it with streamers and tin stars in our living-room on Bleibtreustrasse, back in Berlin our family recognised the festivity, if only half-heartedly, despite it being much less exotic than the Hannuka I only ever read about in books. It's strange how a stamp in a pass-port, thick Gothic characters spelling out the word *jude* that cancel your German nationality, can give you an identity that had never interested me before . . . Ah well, this letter is travelling by airmail, but nobody seems to know for certain when a plane will dare fly across the North Atlantic, or if there will be room for a postbag on it.

I prefer not to tell you what my name and address are — though I do have both, don't worry — until this war is over, and then only if it has a "happy ending". I trust that Salazar's common sense will prevail over any hesitation by Franco, and that between the two of them they succeed in convincing the Germans to keep the Wehrmacht on the far side of the Pyrenees. This is only a postponement, of course: if the Third Reich wins the war, no-one will be able to stop it dominating Europe from the Atlantic to the Urals. But for the moment at least, the neutrality of the entire Iberian peninsula seems secure.

Many refugees have stayed on in Portugal. There are quite a few Wolffs who now call themselves Lobo, and some Mandelbaums who have turned into Almendros. This fits in perfectly well in a country where the "converted Jews" survived the Inquisition with their seven-branched candlesticks wrapped in silk *thales* and hidden in chests tucked away in basements or attics . . . I don't think racial laws would ever work in Portugal. To an even greater degree than in Spain, the Inquisition and its concepts of purity of blood, of new and old Christians, succeeded centuries ago in blurring any possible distinction that the bloodhounds of Aryan purity would have to cross the Straits of Gibraltar to Tangiers or Tetuán if they wanted to find any undisputed descendants of Sem.

All of which is to tell you I do not lament my exile or uprooting, or whatever you wish to call my continued residence in this country, which used to be one of "navigators and poets" and is now living (despite the triumphalist proclamations of what they are calling the "new state") an unending twilight, still gazing out to the Atlantic and turning its back on Europe. My Portuguese is becoming acceptable. I can read more than just newspapers, and I have succeeded in finishing, with only rare consultations of the dictionary, a very minor novel by the writer Eça de Queiroz, *The Mystery of the Sintra Road.* I intend to go on to *The Sin of Father Amaro.*

My most important discovery is Portuguese cuisine. I feel pity and slight disdain when I recall all those *echte mitteleuropäere* who were pining for the hearty stews of Leipzig or Prague when they had in front of them the affordable delights of all the many different ways of serving cod, or even a simple but delicious dish like the *açorda* of seafood. They deserve what they get in the United States.

I have no wish to talk of money or work, the most boring topics imaginable. I can't hope for news from you, as I am refusing to disclose my address on this letter. Perhaps it's better that way: I can imagine the two of you (possibly with a child?) in those idyllic landscapes which Anne used to describe to us beside the Hudson River, barely an hour or more away from Manhattan, that isle which I am told is full of Jews.

See you soon, perhaps.

L'Anonimo Berlinese

14

If it is true that Theo Felder transferred his identity to Franz Mühle so that he could emigrate to the United States, my grandmother found herself blessed with a married name that many people would have considered unfortunate . . . I wonder if she enjoyed upsetting her relatives, deeply rooted in New Hampshire, by becoming Mrs Felder? Be that as it may, it seems her daughter, Madeleine Felder (who became my mother), inherited a destiny along with a surname: aged eighteen, at Woodstock, she met the man who was to become my father, one Aníbal Cahn, born in Argentina. Lovestruck, she followed him to a kibbutz, from which they emerged with all their illusions shattered to open the "Calle Corrientes" pizzeria in Tel Aviv. (Apparently my grandmother referred to her son-in-law as "the kosher pizzaiolo".) It did not take them long to leave Israel: the promised land failed to fulfill the hopes they had invested in it.

My parents separated when I was ten. I can picture them in Buenos Aires, imbued with that sense of failure peculiar to children from well-to-do families who as youngsters embark on adventures from which they return without glory and without having matured in any way. My father, always one to caricature himself, married again, this time to a psychoanalyst I have been careful to avoid; my mother, with whom I lived until I was eighteen, devoted herself to a series of activities vaguely related, I think, to journalism or publicity. These obliged her to spend lots of time at the hairdressers and at openings; if this did not exactly realise her aspirations, it at least filled her days.

I reached the United States too late to know my grandparents, who had died in a car accident at a time when it never occurred to me to be interested in them. My grandmother, unconvinced by the sporadic letters of affection she received from her daughter, made me her only heir, on condition that I get a degree from a North American university. It is thanks to her inheritance that I can occasionally send money to my parents, the constant victims of devaluations, inflation and other Argentine plagues, as well as of their own failings.

I will soon be thirty years old. I know my life is less interesting than that of the people I study. Neither political activism nor sexual exploration offered me the excitement that earlier generations could find in them. It sometimes seems to me that my grandparents, in a pseudo-heroic manner, and my parents, in an almost grotesque parody, used up all the possible curiosity I might have for living adventures rather than reading about them.

Here in Lisbon, for the first time, I have felt something different. I have found myself sitting at a table in a café watching the daylight slowly ebb away, and the ever-changing cast of the city's spectacle, without so much as reading or taking notes. I have been absorbed by my own breathing, my mere presence in this anonymous spot, and have given way to a vague sensuality previously unknown to me, caught up in the happy awareness of simply being alive.

15

The *New York Times* of the 14th of October 1940 reports that on the previous day the Greek steamship *Nea Hellas* docked at the Fourth Street pier in Hoboken, New Jersey. According to the prestigious daily, the ship had rescued an outstanding cross-section of European intellectual life. Among the names mentioned as worthy of the adulation that North Americans profess for celebrity were that of Golo Mann, "son of the famous writer Thomas Mann", who was said to be accompanied by his Uncle Heinrich "also a writer" . . . a warning perhaps that one may be able to change continents but still find it impossible to escape a curse.

The report did not feel obliged to mention my grandparents Anne Hayden Rice and Theo Felder. But now I know (believe? hope?) that Theo Felder (under what name?) stayed on in Portugal, and that the man who assumed his identity was in fact Franz Mühle.

The real Theo Felder — I write the word "real" but have no idea what that adjective means applied to someone who had given up his identity (and what was perhaps still more important in the Europe of that time: his passport) in a loving gesture towards someone who was to use it for the rest of his life, and bequeath this foreign name to my mother . . . I'll begin again: the Theo Felder who disappeared, under who knows what name, in the confused and to me novelesque Portugal of the Second World War must have been sitting in the stalls of the Politeama cinema in Lisbon on that day in May 1945, scarcely a week after the fall of Berlin, a day chosen with exemplary caution by the Portuguese censors as the moment to authorise the first screening of *Casablanca,* a film which only a few days earlier would have violated the New State's scrupulously observed neutrality. I read in the *Diário de Not'cias* that the Lisbon public, doubtless made up mostly of opponents of the Axis, had stood and sung the *Marseillaise* in chorus with the exotic but now forgotten Corina Mura.

(An Argentine friend tells me he witnessed the same reaction in the Opera cinema in Buenos Aires, which was even more audacious given the fact that when the film was first shown on the 6th of May 1943, in the context of Argentina's neutrality that leant towards the Third Reich, there might have been less geographical risk, but it was far more dangerous in regard to the local political situation. This was confirmed by the successful coup launched less than a month later.)

Who else but Theo could have sent that cinema programme to my grandparents? There is no note along with it . . . Did it arrive without any card or line of commentary? Perhaps their very lack makes it all the more eloquent, proclaiming the survival of the man who had once called himself Theo Felder and their memories of him, and also — why not? — alluding ironically to the three friends' story as paralleled by the film plot. In one of the boxes at the Leo Baeck Institute, stuck between successive versions of an unfinished biography of Rosa Valetti and a Lisbon-Estoril train timetable, this programme from the Politeama cinema seems to me steeped in meaning, a footnote displaced five years after their separation, and three years after the only two letters to bridge this absence.

<h1 style="text-align:center">16</h1>

The German bookshop mentioned in my grandfather's notes still exists. I do not know if someone else has taken it over, or if the youngsters who run it are grandchildren of the original owner; the fact is they received my questions not just reluctantly, but warily. No, they do not know of any memoirs by Portuguese writers covering the war years; when I mention *Shicksalsreise* by Döblin or *Ein Zeitalter wird besichtigt* by Heinrich Mann, I can tell they have never heard of these titles, which is understandable; but I also sense that the fact that I mention them arouses their suspicion. There seemed no point in continuing our conversation, so I left without properly checking their shelves, which appeared to be dominated by that week's bestsellers.

In the street I was accosted by a woman who had left the bookshop behind me. I had caught sight of her glancing at the new titles on the centre table. She spoke to me in English, with an accent that sounded more central European than Portuguese.

"I couldn't help overhearing your conversation with those children of the video generation. . . you should pay a visit to Sintra and old Campos' bookshop. I think that's where a lot of the libraries of the exiles who remained in Portugal ended up — he knew many of them."

I scarcely had time to stammer my thanks than my benefactor disappeared with a smile down towards Rua Herculano.

Sintra! The setting for Lord Byron and William Beckford
. . . my guidebook spoke of its microclimate, of the botani-
cal species to be found only in its woods, of a Moorish castle
. . . a train from Rossio station would take me there in less
than an hour.

I was greeted in Sintra by a leaden sky that constantly
threatened a downpour that never materialised. I felt a long,
long way from Lisbon's gentle sunshine. In the distance I
could see trees with constantly changing green foliage as
clouds swept across the sky. The scent of eucalyptus filled
the air. High on the hills, almost completely concealed by
the vegetation, I thought I could see several architectural
follies.

I followed the directions a lottery-ticket seller gave me
and in a street on a steep hillside, squeezed between a store
exhibiting handicrafts and a pastryshop (*"as autenticas queijadas
de Sintra"*), I found the tiny bookshop. Its window immediately put me off: Paulo Coelho and Isabel Allende shared the
spotlight, in between horoscopes and a book of photographs
of Lady Di. The dark interior did not seem to promise
anything more inviting. Despite this, I went in, and got the
impression I was all alone in the long, narrow shop. The
further I advanced from the street, the more interesting the
contents of the bookshelves became, and the thicker the dust
covering them. In by now almost complete darkness I made
out some names that reassured me: Auden and Isherwood,
Journey to a War.

A bare electric light-bulb suddenly came on over my head,
momentarily blinding me.

"Take your time to look around. If you need help, just ask."

The voice was that of an old man sitting, or rather sunk, in a deep armchair where he might have been asleep. His darting, light-coloured eyes looked much younger than the rest of the face, standing out sharply from all the lines and wrinkles.

"Mr Campos?" I asked, not needing to test the limits of my very basic Portuguese. "Do you speak English?"

"Inevitably," he sighed.

I explained I was looking for testimonies about Second World War refugees in Portugal. I did not mention my family ties with the subject I was researching.

"There's no-one left," he answered hastily. "Until a couple of years ago in Torres Vedras there lived some professors who had met Hannah Arendt when she passed through Lisbon. They were the last. There's nobody else left."

This insistence made it hard for me to go on. I thought it would be better to try another tack — how he had got to know them.

"I speak German: I studied in Germany. Years later, during the war, I met some of the refugees in Lisbon — they introduced me to others and so, little by little, I came into touch with many different groups. A lot of them never managed to reach the United States, Mexico or Argentina. They stayed on in Portugal and quite soon they no longer regretted it: they became attached to the country. Some time later, when one of them died, I bought his books: memoirs, history, literature, nothing of any interest to his children. That was how the bookshop began."

Listening to him speak so quickly and assuredly, it seemed to me he must have told this somewhat facile and frankly partial version of his life story many times. Could he be hiding another, less innocent version? I sensed there was an opportunity to convert him into a fictional character . . . at the same time, I realised that at some moment I would end up telling him the story of my grandparents. I had not told anyone about it, and I was afraid of the sympathy this ambivalent stranger might arouse in me. To avoid the risk, I asked him whether he had ever visited the Palace Hotel between 1940 and 1945.

"Of course. And don't go believing all those spy stories invented afterwards. They're simply bad screenplays. Of course there were spies, but everyone knew who they were. A lot of them were double agents. Believe me, there was nothing mysterious about it, only people paid by different governments who wanted to extend their stay in a neutral country for as long as possible so they could eat without rationing and avoid the danger of air-raids."

Once again, as I listened to him, I found myself hatching intrigues around him. A retired spy who for that very reason insists on minimising the importance of spying? His bookshop a meeting place for former spies, still joined together by who knows what earlier loyalties or betrayals?

"There's something I don't understand. How does a young man like you come to be interested in all this ancient history . . . ? Lisbon in 1940 . . . There was nothing romantic or novelesque about it for the people living there in those days . . ."

I would have liked to explain to him that there was a lot of romance and fiction about it, that perhaps one needed not to have lived "there, in those days", but to have been born much later to be able to appreciate, from a radically different world, how romantic and novelesque a simple name and date – Lisbon, 1940 – could be to the imagination of someone like me. But I only succeeded in asking him if he had met, or had heard of, Franz Mühle and Theo Felder. It took him a while to respond. He scrutinised my face with his impenetrable gaze.

"No. Who were they?"

I told him briefly about two German volunteers in the International Brigades during the Spanish Civil War, the number of exoduses they had been through until one, and only one of them, had left for the United States married to a rich heiress.

"And why are you interested in them?"

I was on the point of trusting him with the whole story, but I recovered my sense of caution just in time. I said, which was not a lie, that I had found documents relating to them in a New York library.

"I'm very tired," he whispered after another moment's silence. His voice seemed to have lost all its strength. "I usually open the bookshop a couple of hours a day, no more, just enough for me to feel I have not completely retired. From time to time a friend drops in to see me, but I've lost the habit of keeping up a conversation."

Smiling in a way that carefully avoided separating his lips and risking revealing who knows what dental disaster, he added:

"I'm old."

For one last time I thought that he was lying, as if he might be inventing his age. But it was difficult not to obey this tacit invitation to leave. I thanked him for his willingness to help. I was already headed for the door, and the present-day as represented by the depressing window display, when I heard his voice behind me.

"Take a book, any book, as a souvenir of your visit."

These words touched me more than I could have believed possible. I felt as if Campos had recognised me as a member of the ancient tribe of book people — not a bibliophile anxious to get his hands on rare first editions, but simply someone for whom words printed and kept between two covers are worth any amount of living and worldliness.

I looked around me, disorientated and at a loss. Perhaps to cut short my intrusion, I returned to the copy of *Journey to a War* I had seen on the way in. No sooner had I picked it up than the electric light clicked off, and out of the darkness the old bookseller's voice reached me, close to laughter.

"Those two were looking for a war as well."

* * *

Later that day on the train back to Lisbon, and this morning on the terrace of my *pension*, Campos' last sentence has echoed again and again in my mind. I am not sure that in it he said all I believe I understood. If he did, I would be obliged to come to conclusions I am afraid to accept.

But far from being a source of worry, this doubt is becoming the starting point for a literary project. Will I ever dare to attempt to write it?

I am in no hurry to get back to New York. My ticket expired yesterday. Sometime in the next few days I will go to the local office of the airline company to see if I can extend it. But it is not something I lose any sleep over.

This afternoon I again spent some time on the Santa Lucia esplanade. One of the old chess players greeted me with a silent nod of the head.

NOTE: In writing "Emigré Hotel" I received invaluable help from Lucrecia de Oliveira Cézar, Antonio Rodrigues, and Karsten Witte. The paragraph translated on page 136 is from Jean Giraudoux: *Portugal*, Grasset, 1958.

E.C., Paris, August 2000.